The Good,

The Bad,

and

The Funny

An Anthology of Humorous Tales

by

The Story Forge Writers Collective

Introduction

The Story Forge writers' group has been meeting in one form or another since sometime in 1998. That makes this publication something of a milestone marking twenty years (although it wasn't intended that way and I only realized this salient point as I sat down to write this introduction). Over those twenty years, the faces around the table in the library meeting room – and in fact, the meeting room itself – have changed. Members stay for a while, leave, and sometimes even come back. Sometimes the core group is small, sometimes large. We talk about writing and life and creativity and writing and publishing...and writing. We do freewriting and critique each others' work and help each other brainstorm our way out of tight plot corners. I've often said we're more of a creative support group than anything else, but that's the way we seem to like it.

But occasionally we want to try something new, and the idea of a group anthology blossomed. Since our members cover a broad spectrum of writing interests, we hit on the idea of humorous writing as something that might cross those other genre boundaries and provide a common theme for the book. And of course, it's well-known that humour is the easiest genre to write, right? Right?

The Wilfred Oram Memorial Library in

North Sydney has been our host for these twenty years of meetings, and so in the highly unlikely event this publication generates any funds, we plan to donate them to the library. Libraries contribute so much to our communities and yet often go unappreciated. We truly do appreciate the hospitality and support the library has always offered us.

This book is a group project, and all involved have contributed not only their writing, but their ideas, their input, and their eyes for proofreading. We hope this book will make you smile, make you laugh, and maybe make you want to read more from the authors inside.

- SDR, June 2018

Table of Contents

Big Enough

by Nancy SM Waldman

"LuLu! Talk to me!" Mr. McCormick demanded, shaking me as if I were a lazy child about to miss the school bus.

"My name is JoDee," I said, yanking off my suddenly intolerable lime green wig.

The birthday girl squealed, "She took off her *hair*! She took off her *hair*!"

Tentatively, I pressed a hand to my stinging cheek.

Minutes before, still in my LuLu the Clown costume, I happily lugged a bag full of supplies to my car. The party had gone perfectly *and* the threatening weather had held off.

Putting the bag into the trunk, I felt a tap on my back. *That's Mr. McCormick with my cheque.*

I turned, but instead of payment, I received a sharp slap across the face with what felt like a large, wet fish. My rubber nose went flying, and I followed, landing on the grass next to the street.

Mist began to fall.

Johnny, my new husband, and I moved to Sydney from Dartmouth only a few weeks before. My parents, having a hard time letting their little girl grow up, were not pleased when I told them Johnny's uncle found him a job in Cape Breton.

"What's life without a little adventure, Mum?"

"You're naive, JoDee. It's not adventure you're going to find in Cape Breton."

Dad said, "Even if Johnny's got a job, it won't last. You'll be back in a year. It don't pay to move for that amount of time."

"Why do you have to be so negative?" I asked.

"Experience, doll. Besides, there'll be no work for you there."

That made me mad. I'm only nineteen, but I've already had experience in food services, movie theatres, and I started my own clown business while still in high school.

Within a week after moving to Sydney, I'd organized and decorated our one-bedroom near Wentworth Park. Wedding, baby and family photographs hung on the walls and my collection of crystal figurines made our secondhand furniture look almost new.

Mom called every afternoon. Truthfully, I felt homesick and lonesome, but I'd never let on. The worst thing would be having people back home think I was miserable.

It's going to take time, I repeated to myself a dozen times a day. *Mind over matter!*

Focusing on LuLu the Clown solved several problems: I could make money, prove my dad wrong, keep busy, *and* meet people. I didn't know a soul here except Johnny, unless you counted the tattooed, guitar-playing attendant at the laundromat with whom I'd exchanged a few words.

Johnny came in while I was busy designing the flyer. "You're really going to do the clown thing here?"

Early in our relationship when I first mentioned LuLu, he seemed weirded-out by it and asked where I'd gotten the idea.

"I don't know. Doesn't everyone want to be a clown?"

"No."

"You think I'm strange?" Fear fluttered my tummy.

Johnny was the first boy to pay any attention to me. No one has to tell me that I'm short and more than plump. But when a negative thought enters my mind, I always try to counter with a positive one, such as: *JoDee, you have a pretty face,* or *nice skin,* or *white teeth* or *a friendly personality.* That day, Johnny saved me the trouble by saying, "I don't think you're strange. I think you're sexy."

No wonder I love him.

Now, insecurity surfaced again. "Are you going to tease me about being a clown?"

"I *might* tease you a little." He grabbed me and kissed my neck. "But," he whispered in my ear, "if you want to make extra money by dressing up and scaring little kids, it's fine with me."

I made copies of the flyer in neon colours, cutting flaps along the bottom with my contact information on each one. I bought a new scribbler and carefully noted all my expenses, including the cost of the notebook. Being a complete unknown in town, I decided to charge half what I had in Dartmouth. I posted flyers on bulletin boards and windows all over downtown Sydney. On the way home, I stopped at the laundromat.

"You're a clown?" the attendant asked. I thought of her as Goth Girl. She put down her ever-present guitar and looked the flyer over carefully.

My stomach twisted at the silver knob in her chin. Then I caught a glimpse of silver *in* the girl's mouth. "Yes," I answered, trying to sound upbeat.

"No kidding. Well," she said, now looking me up and down, "it takes all kinds. Sure, tape it up. Why don't you put it on the wall across from the chairs? They won't be able to miss it."

"Great," I said, surprised that this person with black fingernails, purple and fuchsia streaks in her hair and a dragon tattoo on her shoulder was being so helpful. "My name's JoDee."

A small ring slightly deformed the girl's delicate left eyebrow as she said, "I'm Marlene."

"Thanks for your help. I just moved here and don't know many people."

"No problem," she said, picking up her guitar.

As I found a spot for the flyer, she stopped strumming and asked, "What made you want to be a clown?"

I sighed. Why didn't people understand? "The idea just came to me one day when I was in Grade 10 that I could make money by dressing up and entertaining at parties."

Marlene's black-rimmed eyes gave no hint of what she might be thinking. "Do you like it, or is it just a way to make dough?"

"Both."

"What do you like about it?"

"Well, I like kids. I like to make people happy."

"Aren't the kids a pain in the arse?"

I laughed. "Yes! But, they can be sweet, too."

"So it's mostly the dressing up that you like?"

"Why are you asking?"

"Dunno...I always wonder why people choose to do what they do—probably because I don't have a clue what I want."

I nodded, not able to identify with her in any

way.

She went on, "Don't you think it's a little odd and, like, kind of wonderful that in any place in the world, there are people who...like, fill various roles? Like bus drivers or plumbers or court reporters or...clowns! What would happen if no one wanted to be a judge...or a policeman? What if there were a whole generation of only, say...florists and wrestlers."

"Funny," I said, thinking, *Marlene's pretty deep.*

"But the dressing-up thing, *that* I get."

"Oh, I guess you do."

"You don't like my tattoos and piercings."

"Yes I do!"

"Liar. Most people don't. That's part of it for me."

"You want people to dislike you?"

"No. I want people to like me for what's inside, not outside. It's a good way to separate out the phonies."

I wondered if Marlene thought I was one.

"We both dress-up to try out alternate identities," she said.

"I never thought of that. I do feel like a different person when I'm in my costume. But...I don't wear mine all the time."

Marlene's nose ring wiggled. She reached over and encircled my forearm with her hand. I felt her calloused fingertips. "Don't you sometimes wish you could?"

I shrugged.

"Don't you feel a little sad when you have to

take it off and be plain ol' you once again?" My face must have reacted because Marlene quickly said, "I don't mean plain as in 'you aren't pretty.' Of course you are. I mean plain as in 'normal.'"

What's wrong with normal?

Within the week LuLu the Clown had three jobs lined up. I couldn't believe it was going so well.

I repaired my colourfully striped and polka-dotted clown suit I had made in high school. Children always pulled at it, tearing off the ruffles and rick-rack. At one point there were googly-eyes glued all over. The kids loved them, but a little boy in Dartmouth stuffed one up his nose, so I had to take them off. Having paramedics come to a party isn't exactly good for business.

Having a brawl with a competitor isn't either.

The mist changed to drizzle. Mr. McCormick paced back and forth between me and my assailant who had moved up onto the lawn. My chest burned. I tried to stand up, but the grass was slippery and with long clown shoes on, it was like trying to get up while wearing skis. I reached down and pulled them off.

Once on my feet, anger flared. I barrelled toward the slender, grey figure, surrounded by hyper kids. "You!" The cone-hatted woman recoiled. "Why did you hit me?"

Kids scattered.

Mrs. McCormick stepped between us. "Now dear, let's all just calm down."

"She assaulted me! Have you called the police?"

Mrs. McCormick's mouth dropped open. Mr. McCormick interceded. "Ladies, this is my child's birthday. Could you please settle this somewhere else?"

"Settle what?" I shouted, realizing belatedly that I was yelling at my customer. My mind screamed, *No! This can't be happening. This was my best party ever!*

"Would you please leave?" Mr. McCormick begged.

I hadn't taken my eyes off the woman in grey. "What did you hit me with?"

She brought her hand from behind her back. In it was a large rubber chicken, orange and plucked, naked and wet and shiny with the falling rain.

I did my best to squelch it, to hold it in, but it was like holding back a sneeze. A guffaw burst out of my mouth. Hysterical giggles erupted. I was overcome by involuntary laughter.

A rubber chicken. Ridiculous!

At my first Cape Breton party, I had been rusty. I felt off-balance. The next booking, however, I forgot my nervousness half-way through. By the third party, I rocked. Driving home after that one, I noticed blinking car lights behind me. I pulled into a parking lot.

A lanky woman emerged from the small orange car. She was dressed in a costume of undulating metallic colours—silver, blue, gold and copper with streaks of bright magenta. Artfully-applied make-up showed a robot-yet-human mask of brilliant design.

"Wow," I said, "your outfit is great!"

"This is my town."

"What?"

"I'm the clown in this town."

"Heh, heh," I giggled, but the other clown didn't smile. "Well. I— Gosh. I'm just trying to, uh, make some—you know, do my own thing and..."

She stared down, eyes humourless. "This town can't sustain more than one party clown. And, you're undercutting me on price. That's not nice, missy."

"Uh."

"Take a little advice from someone more experienced. Find another occupation. Walk dogs. Be a shop girl. You'll think of something. But you can't be a clown here. I've been doing it a long time. I'm very good. People know me. Save yourself the trouble. Give it up."

The woman, agile as a slinky, slid back into her tangerine-coloured car and drove off. The car door advertised: "Birthday Parties by Silli-Salli the Clown."

"She has no right!" Johnny said, when I told him about the encounter.

"If I'm taking her business because I'm cheaper, then I can see what she's complaining about."

"That's called free enterprise, JoDee. Tough balloons! Don't worry about her. If she's so well-known, then you're no threat to her, right?"

"Well, gosh, no. I never thought of myself as a threat to anyone. I'm just a girl trying to make a few extra dollars."

"If you aren't competing with her, then don't worry."

But I did worry. In fact, I couldn't think of anything else. I decided to take down all the flyers until I figured out what to do.

Marlene wanted to know why I was removing them.

"I just want to make some changes."

"Someone asked me if I knew you. I told them you were a great clown."

"You did? That's so nice of you."

"We clowns have to stick together," she said.

"'We' clowns?" *What was she talking about?*

Marlene looked pleased and said, "Yep. I've been doing a lot of thinking about clowning since you were here. It's so wild, isn't it? Dressing-up in the most outlandish way, acting the absolute fool, whacking other clowns, throwing things! Do you do that?"

"I crack the kids over the head with confetti eggs, and then there's silly string…"

"I'll bet they love it! Kids don't have enough wildness in their lives anymore. That's what's wrong with everyone. LuLu, you've opened up something for me."

"You want to be a clown too?" I asked with immediate concern. The town didn't seem to be big enough for two clowns, much less three.

"Hah! No. I don't want to put on a red nose. I'm talking more metaphorically."

"Okay. Good. I'm glad I could help you out."

I left, feeling a satisfying sense of acceptance from Marlene, even if I didn't understand most of what came out of her mouth.

I already had a party booked before the parking lot run-in with Silli-Salli so, of course, I went ahead with it. The kids gathered around me the whole time, poking their little fingers into the pockets of my costume, checking for candy and treats. Afterward, the parents thanked me, saying I was a real bargain.

Silli-Salli or no Silli-Salli, that party cinched it for me.

This is what I'm good at. It's what I have to do. I reworked my flyers, upping my fee by ten dollars. I retraced my steps, restoring all advertising.

The calls kept coming and I kept working, right up to the McCormick party. The McCormick party, which had been picture perfect right up until Silli-Salli smacked me.

After dissolving into laughter at the sight of the rubber chicken weapon, I looked back at the distraught, confused Mr. McCormick and immediately sobered up at the thought of how utterly ruined everything was. I could feel hysterics changing into hysteria. I turned back to Silli-Salli.

"I'm sorry?" she said in a small voice.

"You hit me!"

"You're taking all my business."

"So, you come to this home where there are children and customers and slap me?"

"I'm desperate. You have to stop."

"No. I do not. That's not the way the world works."

"You do!" Silli-Salli's angular jaw jutted aggressively.

"I do not."

"You have to."

"No, I don't," I argued.

"I'll make you!"

"Just try it."

"Is that a dare?" she said, hand on slinky hip.

"Yes!

"It's not fair!"

"Not fair to me!"

"Stop!"

"No!"

"You little bitch!"

Someone behind me gasped as I dove head first into the deep pool of hysteria that had been waiting. I lunged. Silli-Salli ran, chicken in hand.

Rain poured down, now.

I followed her into the back yard. Abandoned card tables stood holding soggy paper plates with frosting-less, half-eaten cake and disintegrating blobs of Neapolitan ice cream. Ruined crepe paper made garishly coloured puddles on plastic tablecloths. Just ahead, Silli-Salli disappeared behind the screened porch.

I rounded the corner, mowing into her. We went down, crumpling one of the card tables as we fell. Silli-Salli dropped her weapon and squirmed forcefully, pushing against me. I sat on her thighs and, snatching the rubber chicken from the ground, began whacking it back and forth against her skinny, robot arms.

The chicken made an embarrassing burping sound with each thwack.

Silli-Salli went limp, so I stopped.

There were no other sounds. No squeals from children. No cries of protest from parents. I threw the chicken to the ground. It burped one last time and my ears filled with the pounding of my own heartbeat. I looked up to see the McCormicks, the children, and a handful of parents in a semi-circle, staring.

"Daddy," a shrill voice rang out, "are they trying to be funny?"

One of the children pointed a finger and laughed loudly. "Hah-hah!"

I rolled off and Silli-Salli wriggled up on one elbow and shouted, "That's all, kids! Show's over!"

Parents took their children away. Mrs.

McCormick herded the rest of them into the house. "Leave," Mr. McCormick said, through clenched teeth. He followed his wife into the house.

I sat up.

"He didn't pay you, did he?" Silli-Salli had a slab of chocolate icing oozing down her neck.

"No. I expect he forgot," I replied, examining the mud, crepe paper and grass stains on my sodden costume.

"They often do."

"Maybe he was distracted by the grand finale!"

"I lost control."

I struggled up off the ground for a second time. "Clowns cannot afford to go around losing control, can they? And excuse me, Salli-Silli or whatever your silly name is, there's no law that says a town can only have one clown! It's a free damned country and I will be a clown here! Furthermore, your behind is going to be in jail for assault, so this town's going to need me!"

I plodded to the front yard, found my shoes and wig—but not my nose—got in the car and drove away.

It took hours before I stopped trembling. Johnny pampered me, bringing grapes and tiny peanut butter sandwiches while I soaked in a hot bath.

The next morning, my cheek had turned blue and I knew in my heart that I could no longer be a clown. Sure, there was some ranting about calling the police, filing charges, putting "the bitch" in jail, but in the light of day, I realized that would only make things worse.

This woman had friends, a loyal customer base, probably family. How could JoDee, a young girl from away, hope to build a business by prosecuting her competition? How could I hope to compete with someone more experienced, better connected and more professionally costumed? I couldn't. It was over.

I cried all morning.

It was almost time for my mother's afternoon call when I decided to get out of the apartment. I couldn't stand the idea of the conversation my parents would have about their incapable, naive daughter.

I put on make-up to hide my red nose, swollen eyes and blue bruise. Then, I gathered up the dirty laundry and walked slowly to the laundromat, hoping Marlene wouldn't be there. I was out of luck on that count as well.

"Hey there, LuLu. Get any gigs from the signs? I noticed some of your names have been torn off."

"I got a few. Thanks," I said, trying to brush her off.

But it wasn't to be. Marlene, the mod, mad, morbid Goth had transformed into the girlfriend-next-door. She followed me to the washers and planted her elbows on the last one in the row, chattering about her upcoming open mic night at a local bar. It would be her first public performance.

Ordinarily, I would have been interested, but I could barely hear her good news for the problems banging around in my head. "That's really nice, Marlene."

"I was happy to tell people that you're good at clowning. Course, what do I know about you? Nothin'! But, everyone knows that other one..."

"What?" I faced her for the first time.

"God. What happened to you?" Marlene asked, coming over and gently touching my cheek. "Is your old man beating you up?"

"No! He would never do that! What did you mean, the 'other one'?"

"Sor-ry. The other clown. Silli-Salli."

"What about her?"

Marlene gave an expressive shrug and said, "She's the clown kids have had at birthday parties for, hell, generations! From people my age to ten years older and younger, she's been it."

"So?"

"So everyone's seen her *shtick* a million times."

"Her what?"

"Her act. It's always the same. She does this ventriloquist thing that she's pretty good at, but the kids don't get the jokes because they're about things they've never heard of. Mostly parents just don't hire a clown anymore."

16

"But, she has a fabulous costume."

"Huh, well, maybe she got a new one because she used to wear this shoddy old thing that was falling apart, all patched and ridiculous. Sad, really."

I told her just how low this woman had sunk.

"Oh my gawd, LuLu!"

"Uh, Marlene, LuLu is my clown name. My real name is JoDee."

"But, JoDee, what are you going to do?"

"I'm giving it up."

"No! Think of the children! It's your calling."

I stared at her. How had this person become so involved? "Thanks. Really. But you don't understand. I can't muscle my way in. Even if I could get the work, it would ruin her business. I'd make a lot of enemies."

"Don't give up. We'll think of something."

The next morning, I walked into the bathroom only to be confronted with the muddy costume I'd forgotten to take to the laundromat. It lay in a God-awful heap in the corner, a perfect illustration of my collapsed fortunes.

I have been called obsessively optimistic. But, my usual modes of motivating and generating energy and well-being weren't available. I sat at the kitchen table sighing, elbows cross-hatched from the placemat, head on my hands, except when I'd reach up to stroke my not-so-sore-anymore cheek.

When the phone rang, the idea of not

answering it passed through my mind, but I'm not the kind of person who can do that, so I picked it up on the fourth ring. "Hello?"

"Hi. This is Sylvia Fraser...from the McCormick's house? I wanted to apologize again. I want to tell you that I—"

"This is—?"

"Silli-Salli. I don't know what you've decided to do, but I hoped we could talk."

"You're wondering if I've filed charges?" *She's been sweating it out for almost forty-eight hours.*

"Could we meet?"

"Hmm."

"I'm so sorry. I've never hurt anyone before. Are you all right?"

"Someone thought my husband beat me up!"

There was a sharp intake of breath. "Please, meet me. I want to make it up to you."

"Wentworth Park?" I said, after a long pause.

Sylvia arrived after me. Without her makeup she reminded me of the mother of one of my Dartmouth friends. We sat on a bench next to the lake. After hearing what Marlene had to say about this woman and now, seeing her out of costume, I couldn't find my anger.

"I snapped when I saw you there, packing up after a successful party," Sylvia began. "Things haven't been going well for a while."

"I heard."

Sylvia's eyebrows shot up and I saw an

18

exaggerated, theatrical response in the woman's reaction. *I could probably learn a lot from her. She knows how to do ventriloquism.*

She looked out across the lake. A duck with five ducklings paddled along the shore. "I suppose it's well known that I'm washed up. I hoped to squeeze in few more years. Once I pay off my mortgage, I think I can make it."

My throat got tight.

"I never meant to hit you that hard," Sylvia said. "Oh, God, listen to me! I shouldn't have hit you at all! But there you were in costume and...clowns, well—you know."

I nodded. I knew. Clowns are physical. Clowns are absurd. Clowns wallop each other. "We aren't fully ourselves when we're in costume," I said, thinking of Marlene.

"Right! You *do* understand."

"Maybe we could work out something good for both of us," I said, feeling a flicker of hope.

"What do you mean?"

"I'm not sure. Could we combine forces?"

"We can't charge twice as much."

"No, but I'm just starting out. We could split it. 65-35?"

"Just until I get that mortgage paid off?"

"What if we did more than just kid's parties?"

"Like what?"

"Senior Centres?"

"What a good idea! I used to think about doing clowning classes."

"We'd probably be funnier with each other

to work off of."

We brainstormed for an hour. Eventually Sylvia asked, "Does this mean I'm forgiven?"

"Under two conditions. One, teach me everything you know."

Sylvia bowed her head. "That would be my pleasure."

"Two, help me with my costume."

Sylvia laughed. "That would be my duty."

During our afternoon call, I told Mum all about my adventure. After finding a solution to what so recently seemed an insurmountable problem, new confidence bubbled up.

Later, I walked down to the laundromat with my muddy costume. "Hey," I said to Marlene, "where are your purple and pink streaks?"

"Do you like it?" she asked, flipping up the back of her hair with her hand. "It's almost my real colour."

"I sure do."

"I'm starting to feel okay just being plain old me again."

"You'll never be plain. What about your show?"

Marlene excitedly told me all about it. She'd met two guys who wanted her to be in their new band.

Then it was my turn to tell about Silli-Salli.

"You'll be so good for her!" Marlene squealed, giving me a big hug.

"You think?"

"You don't give yourself enough credit. You inspired me to get out of this dump and perform!"

"I didn't know that."

"You know my new band? We're thinking of calling ourselves *The Town Clowns*."

While waiting for my laundry, I took out my scribbler and spent twenty minutes organizing a general plan for pretty much the rest of my life. Optimism buzzed through me, steady and soothing as the hum of the dryer.

This town was big enough for me after all.

*****

Nancy SM Waldman most often writes science fiction or fantasy. After having over a dozen short stories published in Canadian and US magazines and anthologies, she now focuses on novels. They take longer, so please don't ask what she's published lately. Nancy has a long name. As a child, she was called Nancy None because she had no middle name, so her authorial initials—representing gently-used surnames—somewhat make up for this childhood trauma. She saves space by not using periods. When asked her name, she may, after a ten second delay, reply, "It's complicated." Online is no better. Her Twitter handle is nuanc not because she doesn't know how to spell nuance, but because inserting a "u" to her nickname Nanc (soft c at the end, please), made it nu (new) and nuanced. Nancy enjoys subtle complexities. She's a co-founder of Third Person Press, a member of SF Canada, and has been with the Story Forge Writing Group since 2001, when her space odyssey began.

Visit her at http://nancysmwaldman.com.

Mr. Malcolm's Folly

by R. Micheal Magnini

From the private journal of Lord Filbert (Filby) Strathlorne:

On the evening of December 23, in the year of our Lord 1888, Tom and Tim Heath stood in the shadow of a tall hedgerow gazing up at the east wall of a certain Victorian mansion. Said house was located in the country east of London. The ivy-covered red brick was streaked and sliced with moonlight as a sudden breeze blew dry autumn leaves about the garden.

"They say a right distinguished gentleman lives here," said Tom.

"You don't say, eh?"

"A right respectable gentleman, they's say. Ee's a doctor ee is. Ee's got patents and plans, and secret books. Ee's even been to Paris."

"'Ow about that, eh? Makes you kinda proud to be an Englishman."

"Aye, makes my heart real proud. Now, boost me up to that window."

Tim and Tom clambered over the sill and rolled onto the hardwood floor.

"Get off me you oaf!"

"Hey, watch who yer calling an oaf."

"Quiet!"

Tom and Tim looked around the first floor drawing room. The house was dimly lit by wall mounted gas lamps. A very large grandfather clock proclaimed the hour with one sharp peal of its chime.

"Mr. Malcolm said to find 'is diary book first. Then we can have anything that fits in our pockets."

They moved from room to room, amazed and astonished by the doctor's collections of exotic flora and fauna, of bizarre rock crystals, books, manuscripts and papyrus scrolls. Most incredible of all to the interlopers were the timepieces. Every room had clocks, watches, metronomes, timetables, and windup music boxes.

In the rear of the house they found the doctor's study. On his large oak desk lay an open logbook. Tom picked it up, closed the cover, and waved it at Tim, "I've got 'is diary. Ee calls it, 'is 'Chronic Odyssey'".

"'H's place is giving me the creeps. Let's load up and beat it."

Tim and Tom filled their pockets with silver and gold pocket watches, and Tom wrapped a jewelled music box in a scarf. They left the way they had come in, and were even able to close the window behind them.

The hapless brothers waited for hours at the 'meeting place'. Tom sat on the edge of the davenport, his hands on his knees counting his fingers, as he talked.

"We's brung you the book, Mr. Malcolm. So's how about some cash for these nice watches?"

"Boys! Those are mere trinkets. This book," Malcolm said, as he tapped the cover with his knuckle, "is a map to the g-greatest fortune ever conveyed by a dashing rogue and his scoundrels.

"Listen to this: *...I arrived in London on December 24th, 2017. My main objective being the financial district to assess the 'modern' trading systems for stocks, and commodities, and–*

The New Barclays Bank occupied a prodigious space on the bank of the Thames that was no more than an empty field when I departed...

It seems to be of little surprise to learn that the vaults of the New Barclays Bank contain assets counted in the billions of pounds. Upon my return I shall certainly invest heavily in the NBB."

"Uhh, Mr. Malcolm, sir, we're not, that is to say–you want us to rob a bank?"

"Not you, on your own, of course not. We are going to execute the biggest heist in history," he said with a gleaming smile and a maniacal sparkle about his eyes.

"Put that lovely music box on my desk there, and drop all those watches in this box."

"But, Mr. Malcolm, can we's have a little cash to tide us over til the big 'eist?"

Tobias Malcolm drew a one hundred pound note from his vest pocket and stuffed it in Tom's shirt pocket. He patted Tom's chest and said, "There's one more thing I need you to do..."

Doctor Percival Timerson arrived home, entered through his front door and dropped the heavy luggage on the floor. The hour was late, and darkness pervaded throughout his neighbour-hood; he thought of going straight to bed, but decided to have a snifter of brandy first. He had lifted the glass to his nose when he realized something was quite wrong.

Of course, he thought, *the house staff is absent ...*

He searched his office for his journal. His mind raced, his eyes darting back and forth, his breath short he dashed along the hallway to his laboratory at the rear of the house. The heavy door still held secure with dead bolts and padlocks. He found the keys and opened it.

His forbearance fell, as though his blood were draining from his body, as he surveyed the great theft. The rear doors broken and wide open, and the floor deeply scratched where his great advance in science once rested. He walked around the crime scene, gathering his thoughts, gathering evidence. In the wet grass behind his house, the deep divots of horse hooves, and the tracks of the Temporal Engine marked the thieves getaway. The trail faded into the dark of night and shadows of the woods. Any pursuit would be futile before sunrise.

Percival Timerson took a deep exhausted breath. "Damn them." He proceeded to ascend the stairs to the upper rooms of the house. He slumped into a chair next to Radiotronic Telegrapher #3. He rubbed his temples and forehead vigorously with his fingers as he waited for the vacuum tubes and capacitors to heat and charge.

A clock of weighted chains declared the hour as 1:30 a.m. with resonate tones.

He adjusted the frequency tuner to a point marked N.T. His hand quickly tapped the Morse key:

n i c o l a s u r g e n t a s s i s t a n c e r e q u I r e d – c l o c k m i s s i n g ! -- u s e f i e l d s t r e n g t h d e t e c t o r t o l o c a t e
P.T.

Hour after weighted hour wore on his countenance, mood and cognition as he waited through the dark gulf between dusk and dawn, waited for a singular reply.

Sir Percival squinted as rays of sunlight lanced his half-shut eyes. He stood, stretched in the fashion of the new callisthenics, and contemplated his next pursuit. He could wait no longer for Tesla's reply, and so dashed through the corridor to his carriage garage.

"Steady now, girl," he said, pulling himself up into the saddle on his best mare's back. She was a deep chestnut brown with black tail and mane. Sir Percival drew his collar around his neck and trotted Emily out of the carriage house. He nosed her towards the rear of the house and onto the trail of the stolen 'quantum clock'. A disciplined equestrian, Percival Timerson trotted and galloped his steed quickly through the chill air. In an hour he reached the end of the trail–the main road behind the mill.

He travelled along the London road searching, looking for any sign as to which way they had gone. Percival checked each side track and laneway on the way to London in his search. Time, time to think and ask questions, time to speculate and extrapolate. He came to realize that he would need the Constellation of Exceptional Gentlemen to solve this problem.

Sir Percival rode into London town as the sun set behind Westminster Abbey, rooftops glowing orange with the last rays of the day.

Wagons and carriages crowded the streets as the gas lamps were lit one by one by the civil workman in coveralls.

The clapping of Emily's hooves on the cobblestone ceased in front of 66 Baker Street. He sat for a minute apprehending the grey stone building, listening to a melody adagio drift from the upper window, the violin strings in the hands of a master.

He rode on, passing a newsstand papered with the latest headlines of the London Times.

TERROR STALKS WHITECHAPEL
Ripper Strikes Again!

"I fear this will be a weary journey, Emily," said Sir Percival as he gave the horse a nudge. "Up the shire to Lord Kelvin's." The night bloomed with an incandescent sky as he rode up country. *How do I stop this disaster?* he thought, intermittently between dreams of his thick, warm bed and exhausted sleep.

Malcolm leaned his back against the mysterious machine occupying the floor of his rented warehouse. He wore a long, black waistcoat with a high collar. His arms crossed across his chest, his head tipped forward hiding his face under the shadow of his green and black Scotch bonnet, he pondered his fates.

"Mr. Malcolm, sir, we was wunderin if we's could have's more cash?" said Tom. "We's spent the hundred quid on renting the wagon for the boost."

"Boys, boys, boys!" he declared loudly walking around the metallic and crystalline apparatus. He ran his hand along its chassis admiring the detailed workmanship.

"We are on the brrrink of the greatest moment in history!"

"But, Mr. Malcolm, we's brung you the sleigh like you asked and–"

"Hush Thomas. Listen to me, boys," he said in a whisper. "I know Timerson very well. We were colleagues at the University of Edinburgh. The theory of Time Displacement is mine. The board of directors, those tea-sipping old ladies, they–well, I was too brilliant for them. To save their precious reputation they dismissed me for... for–outrageous fantasy!

"Then, you know, boys, what happened? Timerson stole my work and built this wonderful machine."

"Sir, Mr. Malcolm, I was wonderin, if you would loan me a few quid, you know, against the next job and all," said Tim.

Malcolm stood facing them. He said sternly, "Listen boys, we all want our payday. And I'm going to tell you how and when we do it. For now, listen..."

Using pieces of schoolhouse chalk he wrote quadratic equations, exponential graphs, calculus and the Mobius matrix on the wall of the warehouse.

"...so it is proven that the diffraction of the time wave equals 0. Essentially, we will arrive and return in fractions of a second."

Trying not to appear too dim, Tom said, "Err, very impressive sir, and quite right I'm sure. I'm just not seeing the payday, sir."

"Very well my Tom and Tim, but let's call you Tick and Tock, shall we? Here is High Street," he said, drawing a sketch map of London on the wall. "And right here we will empty the vault of the New Barclays Bank."

Tom sat nonplussed, blinking rapidly. Tim squinted trying to read the chalk marks. "Mr. Malcolm, sir, I knows that street and there's no bank at that spot. I knows it's a field. They's play ball there every Sunday."

The brass doorknocker resonated with a thunderous boom against the thick oak door. Moments later the door swung slowly open, and a little, neatly dressed man stood in the frame. Sir Percival Timerson stood facing him, raindrops dripping from the brim of his hat.

"I must speak to Lord Kelvin, immediately."

"Are you referring to the Lord of the house, William Thompson, sir?" replied the diminutive man, well dressed in tweed.

"Yes Merlion," huffed Percival, "tell William it is of grave importance!"

"I'll see to it right away, sir. Please warm yourself by the fire."

Sir Percival stood staring into the glowing coals, the small yellow-orange flames rippling across the heap, the warm radiation penetrating his cold flesh; his eyes slowly closing as his thoughts drifted to sleepy meadows.

A warm and friendly slap on the back woke him. "Percival Timerson! What a pleasant surprise!"

"Good to see you, William," he said, "I wish it were during more favourable times."

"What seems to be the trouble my good friend?" inquired Lord Thompson, "Please, join me in the laboratory. I'm eager to learn all about your latest experiments." The future Lord Kelvin walked with Sir Percival through a great arched hallway of plaster and polished wood, illuminated by thin, glowing glass pipes along the crease of the ceiling and wall.

Lord Thompson's laboratory existed in a state of constant flux. The two-story 'greenhouse' behind his mansion still retained its glass roof and the stars twinkled through it.

"You look inwards and outwards, Lord Kelvin. What have you discovered through your telescope?" asked Percival, looking up at his observation platform. The stairs were worn and the chair carried a large wool blanket.

"Why, Mars, of course. The Canali," said Lord Thompson, "but, you certainly didn't come all this way, on this rainy night, to sky gaze?"

"I need your help."

Sir Percival ambled up several steps of the observatory, stopped and sat facing Lord Thompson.

"You know of course, of the experiments that occurred in my garden? The minor temporal anomalies, which occurred during the dimensional tests of the ether-force, were then amplified by the field effect generator that I designed. Eventually, I built a temporal engine that traverses, and carries material on the meridian of time. The discovery was astounding and perplexing. I recklessly pressed ahead and voyaged to a future time. I discovered many things, some marvellous and some quite disquieting. As a good scientist I kept careful notes and observations."

"I'm delighted to hear of your amazing discovery dear Percival!" extolled Lord Thompson.

"It has been stolen," he said, clenching his fists and staring at the floor.

"I dare say, what a hideous offence," declared Lord Thompson, "Of course I will assist you. Do you have the resources to construct another engine?"

"Yes, of course," said he softly, "but if the machine is used... if it is activated and used by the corrupt and ignorant the outcome could be catastrophic...

"If they manage to initiate the engine and delve into the future, we are all in peril. Any part or piece of the future that returns is extremely dangerous. Most dangerous of all is knowledge. Be it books, formulas, medicines, philosophies or religions, any would intersect with this timeframe and alter the course of history and evolution in vast and unknowable ways. Wars out of time could devastate the planet, or cause our extinction."

Lord Thompson summoned his housekeeper. "Mary, would you be a dear and bring Percival tea?"

"The paradox equation becomes very important. Anything that changes the past, changes the future. The future can be re-written and the past unalterably changed. All the wonders of the future must remain there. We must find the machine before they can use it!"

Lord Thompson looked down in contemplation as silence descended upon them. "You have travelled to the future and returned. You brought knowledge with you. I am torn now between the desire to learn what you have discovered and the obvious necessity of non-interference with the time stream. "It occurs to me, Doctor Timerson, that you are the paradox."

"What chances have we then, Lord Kelvin?"

"We will find your machine. Let us calculate the most probable route for the conveyance of your engine."

Thompson stood at his chalkboard quickly dashing off mathematical functions as Timerson provided the distances, timeframes and physical dimensions of the engine. Twenty minutes later, Thompson drew a circle on the board, and tapping it, said, "The warehouse district of the Thames docks. Your engine is there."

"That is a large area to search, and we should avoid involving the constabulary."

"Yes, yes, of course. We will acquire the help we need from the Gentleman's Club. Join me for a dram, and we'll pursue the vagabonds in the morning. The rain is quite heavy now."

They clicked their glasses together, and said in unison, "To the Gentleman's Club!"

On December 24, within the confines of the rented warehouse, Tobias Malcolm sat pensively staring at the instruments in the dash of the carriage. With the leather seat firm and comfortable he studied the three clock faces and three levers; he watched Tim and Tom play Black Jack for two-pence; he gazed down at Timerson's Chronic Logue book nested on his lap.

"Not a word!" exclaimed Malcolm.

Startled, Tom said, "Sorry, sir."

"Not a word in this anecdote about how to pilot this devil's device," said Malcolm. Fumbling under the seat, he found a hand lever and pulled it up. It hummed like a nest of bees; as it grew louder a mirrored sphere behind the chair began to slowly rotate.

Malcolm sat upright, twisting in his seat to look at the spinning orb. He turned and reached for the dashboard, then stopped.

"Boys! Come over here and see what a magnificent man's machine looks like!"

Squinting and tucking their chins, Tim and Tom approached the side of the carriage. "How does it move? It 'as no wheels an' no horse."

"How does it move? Ha!" howled Malcolm. "It moves through tomorrow!"

"I dun know, sir, if we might get a little cash today before we go to tomorrow?"

"You are absolutely right my mathematically-challenged minion!"

"Sir?"

"Ascend the chariot of tomorrow. Sit here," said Malcolm.

"Timothy, you wait there," he followed, "until we return."

Tim's face crumpled in confusion. Tobias pushed on the first lever slightly with his index finger. The sphere rotated with increasing speed emanating a brilliant ultra-blue light. After a brief moment he released the lever.

Tom and Tobias neither felt nor saw any difference.

"'S about time! You's 'ad me sittin' 'ere all day and it's night now," croaked Tim. Malcolm sprang from the carriage and seized Tim by his shirt, "What did you see?"

"Just the blue light, sir. It goes bright, then faint, then bright again. That's all sir."

"Wait here," replied Malcolm as he leapt back onto the carriage. He pushed the lever forward, the dash clocks moved at different rates, the warehouse filled with ultra blue-violet light, and he released the lever.

The warehouse was quiet and empty. Dust covered the floor and storage boxes. Malcolm's wall sketch was faintly visible.

"What happened, Mr. Malcolm?" said Tom, not hearing himself through the ringing in his ears.

Malcolm looked at the chronometer in the dash: 4 yrs 1 m 18 days. "Do you see that, Tommy? That's four years of dust in less than four seconds!"

Malcolm leapt out and onto the floor. He adjusted his bonnet and said, "Wait here. Stay quiet. I'll return shortly." A bright beam of sunlight crossed the empty warehouse as Malcolm slipped out the door.

On the street Malcolm was startled by the whirring bangs and clatter of a motorized vehicle that nearly hit him.

Tom walked around the engine and the warehouse; he found the deck of cards where he had left them an hour ago–four years ago?– covered in fine dust. The more he thought about it the more his head hurt.

The warehouse door banged open and Malcolm strolled in holding a newspaper in his hand. His countenance was confident and he wore a wide smile.

"Don't dotter there, get in the carriage. We shall fly backwards now."

As Malcolm considered the control levers, Tom read the front page of the London Times as it lay on the seat next to him.

February 2, 1892

RIPPER ELUDES HOLMES

Inspector Holmes set a snare for Jack by disguising himself as a prostitute, and wandering the alleys of Whitechapel, Sunday night. The cunning inspector succeeded in baiting the lunatic into a confrontation behind the apothecary. In desperate hand-to-hand combat, Inspector Holmes received superficial knife wounds before the Ripper ran off into the cold, chill night.

Inspector Holmes is recovering and has said he will 'capture the killer within a fortnight.' Meanwhile in Whitechapel....

A brilliant blue flash flooded his eyes and suddenly they were back to the starting point next to a dumbfounded Tim.

After a leisurely breakfast, Lord Thompson and Sir Percival set off in the Lord's closed carriage to the Gentleman's Club located far to the north of London. Percival and William discussed many things concerning the Paradox Peril, and ways to circumvent disaster.

In the late afternoon, a sturdy hand on his shoulder awakened Percival. "We've arrived dear Percival."

William and Percival disembarked the

carriage, tipped the driver, and as it pulled away, passed through the double gothic door entering the Gentlemen's Club. The main lounge, of course, was infused with pipe smoke and several groups of men sitting in heavy, upholstered chairs were in animated discussions.

"It may take us some time to rouse them from their comfortable chairs, my friend. But bear with me, be patient, and we will regain your enterprise!" encouraged Sir Percival's companion.

Lord Thompson and Sir Percival Timerson checked their tall hats, and coats.

"So good to see you, Lord Thompson!" blurted Cromwell as he seized Thompson's hand. "Come sit with us! We're discussing the merits of astrophysics in light of the recent discoveries."

"I have a great tale for you Cromwell. One that you will want to hear," retorted Thompson, "Come, let's sit together"

Seats were acquired in a secluded corner of the main room. Sir Percival gazed about the club as Thompson expounded the dilemma to Cromwell. He overheard a portly gentleman mutter, "Dreadful. Absolutely dreadful...this Ripper business."

In another corner were esteemed men of the literary class, including a young man with a wide moustache, a convincing voice and a futuristic twinkle in his eye. Across the room, through an open doorway Sir Percival could see a lecture being given by the Italian Astronomer Giovanni Schiaparelli.

Sir Percival felt light-headed, sounds becoming muffled and indistinct; he watched Cromwell's lips move when a porter placed a serving of tea on the table. The fragrance of sugared Ceylon tea opened Percival's eyes and he heard Thompson say, "Schiaparelli has heard of our dilemma and has offered to join our search of the east London district."

"Splendid, I say. We deploy at the dawn then," replied Cromwell.

"Percival, you are in need of food and rest. Gentlemen, let's retire to the dining room then," said Thompson as he stood.

"Shouldn't we pursue the thieves immediately?" urged Sir Percival.

"Nonsense, my good man. Our forces will be stronger in the morn."

On the morning of December 25, Mr. Malcolm's magnificent men, Tim and Tom, Tick and Tock, pushed the warehouse doors open. In the east, a thin red line creased the horizon, the air chill and quiet. The docile mare was cinched up to the flatbed hay wagon while Tobias frantically sketched and calculated on Timerson's journal.

"Here," said he, proffering a neatly drawn map, "take the engine to this exact spot. And before you do, cover it with that." He pointed quickly at several bales of straw against the wall.

As the dawn broke over the smoky skyline, Tom and Tim walked their 'hay wagon' away from the warehouses towards the empty fields along the Thames. Upon arrival, some two hours later, Tom and Tim sighted Malcolm on one knee gazing up at the sun through a sextant. He stood and pushed a long stake into the soft earth. "Aye–over here, boys!" exclaimed Tobias waving frantically.

"Push! Put yer backs into it!" cried Malcolm as they dragged and manoeuvred the engine into exact position.

"This is it, lads," he said, gingerly pressing his palms together. "Brush off this straw. Tick, you must wait here with the wagon. Tock, you ride with me."

At half past noon on December 25th, Tobias Malcolm pulled the starter lever and as the spinning sphere brightened he advanced the forward control lever. Tim shaded his eyes with his hand during the machines transition.

"Oy! I should've asked when they's was comin back!"

Five remarkable men disembarked from two large, black coaches at the head of the warehouse district. Cromwell and Thompson set out along Front Street, while Sir Percival, Schiaparelli, and Mr. Wells proceeded up Shore road.

Peering in windows, wall cracks and open doors, the troupe of marvellous gentlemen hurried in their effort to find the missing craft.

Giovanni sported a unique set of eye glasses, their lens and prisms adjusted at a finger's touch. He surveyed the outer walls, searching for differences in colour.

Sir Percival, a rare and peculiar man, tugged on a gold chain that dangled from his vest pocket. At its end, a double-faced pocket watch spun. He held it flat in his gloved hand and gazed at the compass needle; he then turned the watch over and read the time.

Mr. Wells, following Schiaparelli, presented him with a great curiosity about astronomy. "Is it your opinion that the canali of Mars is not natural? Could this phenomenon be engineered? That is to say, could intelligence be behind these artefacts?"

"Meester Wells, if indeed some other, knowledge, created these immense structures surely they are ancient and extinct. You know that Mars is without water?"

"Yes, of course, the water. If they were jealous of our water…"

"Avanti, avanti! I've-a found something," exclaimed Giovanni.

Sir Percival pocketed his watch, crisply turned and trotted to Giovanni's side. The three exceptional men stood staring at a vacant warehouse, its doors shuttered. Mr. Wells said, "Allow me," and proceeded to pry one side open. Percival held an electric lamp in his hand, illuminating the dusky interior. The beam fell on a bare floor, a few wooden crates against board and batten walls.

Doctor Percival strode to the centre of the floor and drew his pocket watch. The compass needle swept quickly from N to S and S to N. "It was here!"

"Perhaps they have left clues. I suggest, gentlemen, that we search carefully," insisted Mr. Wells.

Doctor Percival held his watch chain in the air before his face. He examined the faces of the double-sided watch as it rotated... the clock hands suddenly stopping, then springing to a different hour of the clock.

"Heaven help us, gentlemen. They have engaged the Engine."

Mr. Wells had found the deck of cards, and Schiaparelli stood an arm's length from a dingy wall near the back. He adjusted his array of lenses until the image was clear. "Meester Timerson. I have discovered a treasures map on thees wall."

At that moment, Lord Thompson and Cromwell entered the warehouse.

The group of five remarkable men gathered before the chalk scuffs that resembled the layout of London town. "An X marks the spot," intoned Mr. Wells.

"Can you decipher this, Percival?" asked Lord Thompson.

Sir Percival, alert and rested, struck the X with his cane. "Why here?" said he, and closing his eyes entered a meditative trance. The future memories whirled about in his mind like a sandstorm; he recalled finding his house still

43

standing, albeit boarded up and abandoned as he emerged in the twenty-first century. He felt himself walking the streets of future London and startled by all the men without hats. After making clothing adjustments, he visited libraries and banks – including the New Barclays Bank on the Thames!

"Lord Jesus," gasped Percival.

"What is it man?" cried Mr. Wells.

"The Paradox, William, the Paradox!"

The group of exceptional gentlemen listened intently as Doctor Percival tried to explain the dilemma. "There is only one Engine made of brass, onyx, obsidian and quartz. It has trans-positioned in 1887 to the year 2017 – the maiden voyage. All of this is evident in my journal. The scoundrels! Should the Engine transpose from 1888 to the same spacetime in 2017, it would mean --."

"Yes, yes I see it," exclaimed Thompson, "one machine can not occupy two distinct places at the same moment!"

"It may be too late, however our only chance is to intercept them at this mark."

Enveloped in the scintillating blue light of the Temporal Engine, Malcolm fixated on the dashboard chronometer as it flickered and flashed, the numbers accumulating rapidly while Tom gripped the brass rail with all his strength. The voyage through one hundred twenty nine years had been compressed into six minutes of ship time. Malcolm slowly depressed the lever, the humming of the Engine subsided and the violet light shrunk around them.

"If my calculations are correct, we are about to emerge into the heart of the world's richest bank."

The Engine pitched and fell hard onto a concrete floor throwing Tom from the rig. Inside the vault, small green and blue bulbs flickered up and down racks of steel boxes, and a dim light shone from glass panels on the wall.

The dash chronometer settled at: 2017:12: 25.

"What's this?" remarked Malcolm. He approached the flickering glass panel which displayed an unfamiliar algorithm in multiple colours. As Tobias read and interpreted the charts and graphs he exclaimed, "Acch!"

He read:

The Market is closed. It will reopen in 16 hours, 56 minutes. Cryptocurrencies:
Bitcoin: High: $14,014.00 Close:$13,927.47 U.S. dollars

"Mr. Malcolm, sir, where's all the gold and money?"

"It's here. It's all here," he sniffed. "But we can't take it with us!" he howled.

"Mr. Malcolm, sir. Can we go home now?"

With wretched despair, Tobias pulled and

pushed the travel levers and a great blue light carried them away.

At four p.m., GMT, the Temporal Engine emerged out of the thin blue air on December 25th 1888, in the empty field on the Thames. Tobias furiously beat the dashboard with his fist. Tim sat on the hay wagon looking pensive and quietly uncomfortable. As the machine fell quiet, men leapt out of the hay, and others ran out from behind the wagon.

"Seize him!" shouted Lord Thompson.

"The Temporal Engine was surrounded by a band of extraordinary gentlemen. Unlike those in the future, these men wore hats. Two Empire top hats, two black Bowler hats, a Derby hat, a Deerstalker cap and two Custodian helmets all surrounded Tobias Malcolm.

As Inspector Holmes and two constables escorted the thieves away, Tom was overheard to say, "Mr. Malcolm, sir, could you spot me ten quid? You know, just to tide us over 'til next time...?"

"We are all discreet gentlemen here. In the interests of Her Majesty and Her Empire, let's keep this little incident between us, shall we?" proclaimed Cromwell.

"And whatever will become of your Engine, dear Percival?" asked Lord Thompson.

"This remains to be seen, my Lord Thompson. It shall henceforth be called the Paradox Engine," replied Percival, "and not everyone is ready for the future."

"I concur. And I believe you deserve a title. I should think we should call you, Lord Time."

"May I offer another moniker," injected Mr. Wells, "perhaps he should be called the Time Traveller?"

And, it is presumed that on Tuesday, the 26th of December in the year of our Lord two thousand and seventeen, the manager of the New Barclays Bank could not explain the appearance of straw inside their locked and fortified vault.

*****

R. Micheal Magnini is the author of numerous articles published in several magazines; he has written two books in the field of beekeeping; he has also edited the late, great SF anthology *North of Infinity*; and currently is burning the midnight oil writing a collection of SF stories.

An expatriate from Ontario, he lives and works in Scotch Lake on his farm where he shares life with Jennifer, Freya, Alphonso, Tipster, and a host of other creatures.

He enjoyed the friendship, and tough love, of the Hamilton Writers' Workshop during the nineteen-nineties (helping to create the anthology: *Your Baggage is in Buffalo*). He presently has been a member of the North Sydney Writers group for two years.

Sausage, Eggs, and Bacon

by Jo-Ann D. MacDonald

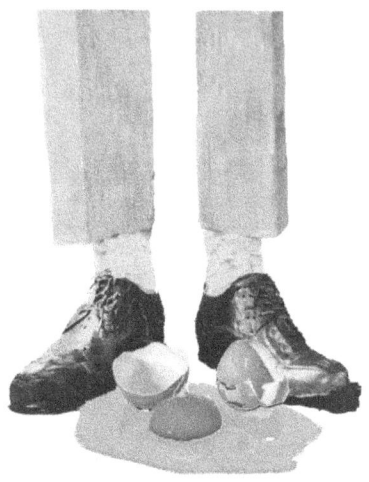

Before he even opened his eyes, Jack Fraser knew the rain had finally given up. He rolled his weary body over. The bed creaked but his joints didn't—a very good sign. He opened one eye first and then the other, blinking away the sunshine that streamed into the room. He forgot to close the curtains last night.

He smiled for the first time in a week and ran his hands through the wisp of white hair on the top of his head.

The grumbling in his belly reached his ears from under the covers. First order of the day — *breakfast.*

He sprang out of bed and looked out the window. It was a glorious day. He threw up the sash and looked down at the street below. The warmth of the sun and the earthy scent of moist earth rose up, filling his nostrils and putting a smile on his withered face. Patches of the paved street below were drying up where the sun's rays lazily beamed down. A car went down the road—a little too fast, Jack thought. It hit one of the lingering puddles, spraying up a wall of water and for a brief second only, broke into a rainbow of colours.

He stretched, sighed contentedly and proceeded to the kitchen. The rainy, grey weather of the past week had been depressing as hell. So depressing that he hadn't even cooked himself a decent meal. But today was going to be a good day. He felt great and decided then and there to celebrate by treating himself to a good breakfast followed by a little bit of writing poetry.

"Sausage and eggs," he suddenly said aloud. "That's what I want. Sausage and eggs."

He opened the refrigerator, hunched over and stared at the mostly bare shelves.

"Good morning Whiskers," he said to the cat. He gave her head a gentle pat as she slinked between his ankles, purring. She let out a raucous meow that could possibly mean only one thing: *feed me!*

"You'll get yours soon," he assured her, and scruffed her affectionately behind her ears. Then he took out the carton of eggs and a package of sausage and put them both on top of the counter.

He opened the carton of eggs and was dismayed to see only two eggs left. He thought for a moment and tried to remember the last time he had bought eggs. He drew a blank. That was one of the drawbacks of being an old guy; the memory wasn't always so great.

He lifted the cardboard carton and checked the side, scrunching up his eyes to find the best before date. He held it close to his face and then at arm's length. He deciphered some blurry numerals that looked possibly like May 20.

"That can't be right," he muttered, going back into the bedroom to retrieve his reading glasses. He put them on and took another look at the side of the egg carton. *May 20.*

"Son of a gun." He looked at the calendar. They were expired over a month ago. His belly grumbled again. He'd been really looking forward to sausage and eggs. In fact, sausage and eggs were all he could think about now.

He opened the carton of eggs again and took another another look. He even took a whiff of the brown shells. How bad could one-month-expired eggs be? He shrugged and decided he was hungry enough that the eggs were worth the risk.

He reached for the frying pan and stopped, horrified. The cat was on the countertop.

"Whiskers!" he shouted. He pulled the yowling cat off the tray of raw, half-eaten sausage just as the eggs dropped to the floor with a *thud-crack-splat.*

Jack groaned. He sighed and resigned himself to not having his sausage and sunny-side-ups after all. He went to the cupboard and took down a box of Rice Krispies, his breakfast staple. The box felt light in his hand, so he gave it a little shake. Almost empty. *Not much snap crackle and pop in there,* he thought, but poured the contents in a bowl anyway. The crumbs barely covered the bottom. And when he pulled out the milk carton—expired.

There was no avoiding it. He would have to the grocery store.

With a glance at the sunshine outside, and the pleasant breeze blowing through the window, he thought it wasn't a bad day for a walk anyway.

The Value-Mart wasn't far, just a short jaunt down the street. It was a relatively small grocery store and he'd be in and out of there in a wink. He'd come right home and cook up his sausage and eggs.

He wore his favourite cardigan. The day was warm and only promised to get warmer. Jack felt better already. The expired food, the cat—it was all a minor setback. He skipped over a puddle, whistling a song and loving the day.

As he approached the Value-Mart, the automatic doors sprung wide open. He stood in front of the entranceway, not sure what it was that made him hesitate. A strange, niggling feeling in his gut told him that something wasn't quite right. He decided he was being silly and chalked it up to hunger.

Minutes later, he realized the source of that niggling feeling.

He picked up a shopping basket just inside the door and started toward the eggs. Passing by the cereal aisle, he remembered needing Rice Krispies. Better pick up some cat food too, he thought grumpily, even if that danged Whiskers already had her fill for the day.

As he reached for the box of cereal, he stopped, hand midway in the air.

Her.

Nellie was walking past the aisle on her way to the dairy section.

He grabbed the box of Rice Krispies, threw it in his basket and took off in the opposite direction. He weaved his way through the aisles, peeking around corners, desperate to avoid–*her.*

The next time he spotted her, she was walking toward the meat section. He tucked in behind the aisle, wiping his sweaty palms on the front of his cardigan. She walked smartly past in her practical shoes, silver hair tucked behind one ear with a bobby pin, a grocery basket hooked in the crook of her arm.

She gave Bob the butcher a brilliant smile and a cheerful hello.

"Mmph," Jack grumbled under his breath. Of course. She'd always had a thing for Bob.

He darted back to the cat food, fighting to control his nervousness. His hands shook as he put the cans of cat food in his basket and his heart thumped wildly in his chest.

Sausage and eggs kept him going. He found his courage, took a deep breath and made his way to the chilled shelves of eggs.

Above the eggs was a sign that read, "Sausage half price with the purchase of eggs."

It must have been a good sale, there were only two cartons left.

He glanced over his shoulder. He had to be stealthy. The meat section was just around the corner.

He gingerly picked up the eggs and was about to carefully place them into the grocery basket when a sudden — yet very familiar — braying of laughter reached his ears. Startled, he dropped the carton. The eggs hit the floor. For the second time in less than an hour, he had clear, yellow goop oozing in a large circle around his feet.

People stopped and stared. He could only stand there, rooted to the floor of Value-Mart. Embarrassment rose up from the base of his neck to the top of his balding dome, her chortle still ringing in his ears.

Of course, as long as he stood there, he could still hear her. She was carrying on, flirting with the butcher, her laugh tormenting him. He wanted to run, hide, get away from here, get away from this store. Back to his apartment. But dammit, he wasn't one to give up. And he really wanted those sausage and eggs.

A pimple-faced youth wearing a Value-Mart apron approached him with a mop and bucket.

He cleaned up the smashed eggs and helped to restore some of his dignity.

With the mess cleaned up and the last carton of eggs in his basket, the old man made his way toward the meat section. Sausage was on his mind and sausage he would get.

Bob the butcher was stocking up on bacon, loading it from the meat cart to the shelf. The sign above his head reminded shoppers, "Sausage half price with purchase of eggs."

Thankfully, there was no sign of *her*.

"Hey, Jack," said Bob, as Jack approached the sausage bin. "I see you have your eggs. The sale was a huge hit."

"I noticed," said Jack, eyeing the one package of sausage left. "Glad I got here in time. I've been thinking about sausage and eggs for breakfast all morning!" he reached into the bin but stopped as Bob leaned in toward him.

"Hey, Nellie was by earlier. She was asking about you."

"Asking? About me?" Jack felt a lump in his throat. He was confused. Why would she be asking Bob about him?

Bob must have noticed how pale he'd become. "Give her a chance, Jack," he said. "Get to know her. You'd like her. Besides, she's a great cook."

"Great cook?" he muttered. Like a zombie, he stared, unsure of what to say, think or even how to react.

"Yep. I think she has a thing for you," Bob

gave him a wink.

Jack looked around awkwardly, slowly coming to his senses. "Uh, yeah." His voice was more high-pitched than usual. "Okay, Bob. Thanks for the heads up." The last thing he needed was Bob the Butcher playing matchmaker. And with *her*!

Bob put the last package of bacon on the shelf and Jack gave him a wave as he wheeled his cart into the back room.

Like a gull, the old man moved in, seizing the package in a satisfying death grip.

He realized there was an issue when he tried to put the package of sausage in his grocery basket. Someone else's hands were on it.

Nellie's hands.

Onc second passed, then two before he had the gumption to look up into her face.

"Looks like you're having bacon today," she said sweetly, grinning from ear to ear.

He shook his head. "I don't want bacon." His hands were sweating, his heart pounded.

Just then, Bob came through the back room doors with a another cart full of ground beef. He saw the conundrum with the sausage— Jack and Nellie in their tug of war. "Sorry," he said. "That's the last package until tomorrow."

She smiled at Jack sweetly once again, "you wouldn't deprive a lady of her sausage, would you, Jack?"

The butcher snickered as he walked around them to the far shelf.

Jack yanked the meat toward him, hoping she was just toying with him. He had his hands on it first, after all. "Jack, do be reasonable," she said, clutching the bangers tightly.

"I am being reasonable," the old man explained, trying to sound calm. "My hand was on it first!" His voice had risen several octaves. People were staring—again. He had to get a grip.

Normally he would have gladly let go. He'd always given Nellie what she wanted before *the incident.*

He dropped his voice, almost to a whisper. "It's just…I don't *want* bacon."

"You don't want bacon?" she asked, smiling provocatively and taking her turn yanking the sausage toward her own basket.

Jack held fast with gritted teeth. "No. I. Don't. Want. Bacon." It was a point of principle now.

Keeping a hold of the package, Nellie stopped and gave him a curious look. She lowered her voice. "Jack, is everything okay? I thought we were friends."

"I thought we were friends, too," said Jack, sparing a glance in Bob's direction where he continued to stack packages of ground beef. "Maybe *Bob* can help you get what you want."

"I beg your pardon?" she replied with a sharp intake of breath, a delicate hand on her chest and a highly affronted look on her face. "What is that supposed to mean?"

Bob the butcher broke in at this point. "I think he's still a bit sore from writer's group, Nellie."

"Writer's group?" she exclaimed, looking from Bob the Butcher to Jack. "Why, Jack hasn't been to Writer's Group for months!"

"Since Valentine's Day," said Bob.

"That's right," she said, turning to Jack. "You read your poem. I've often wondered why you never returned."

Red heat rose up Jack's collar and over his cheeks. The hours he had spent writing that poem, perfecting it. It was romantic and meaningful, expressing his soul — his most intimate thoughts. *No, of course he didn't write it for her!* It was just an exercise. For writers group. Nothing more. Yet she shredded his soul and left it on the library floor.

Nellie drew her breath in sharply. "I hope I didn't upset you when I mentioned that 'rove' doesn't rhyme with 'love'," she said.

The sheepish look on his face gave her his answer.

"Oh, Jack, I really do love that poem...I even have a copy of it on my fridge. You can ask Bob." She looked to the butcher for confirmation.

Jack glanced reluctantly at the butcher who nodded, agreeing with her.

"I thought you wrote it for Nellie, to be honest," Bob interjected.

"I thought you stopped coming to group because you didn't like my brother. You kept giving him funny looks at the meeting," said Nellie, her brows furrowed.

At this point, both men looked totally confused.

"Your brother?" questioned Jack. "I didn't even know you had a brother!"

"Whaddaya mean he doesn't like me?" Bob demanded at the same time.

Both men's jaws hung open in surprise, their eyes wide. Neither could conceal their astonishment.

"Well of course I have a brother!" Nellie exclaimed. "Didn't you know, Jack? Bob...Bob here is my brother!"

Jack looked back and forth between the two of them. "Ohhhhh," he said as understanding crossed his face.

The first time Jack had met Nellie was at the library. Interestingly enough, they both had their hands on the same book, *Poetry for Beginners*. At that time, Jack was a complete gentleman. He wasted no time in letting her have the book. When she invited him to attend Writers Group the following week, he was surprised to find that he was excited and looking forward to seeing her again. He was taken aback and disappointed to see her walk in with another man—Bob the butcher.

Of course, she was her usual friendly self— she smiled and batted her eyes at Jack. Bob was friendly, too but kept a close watch on Nellie before escorting her to his car at the end of the night. What was Jack supposed to think?

Jack looked down at the package of sausage held firmly between them.

"Well then," said Nellie. "This can only go one of two ways."

He narrowed his eyes shrewdly. "Go ahead."

"I can stand here and make a scene...."

"Or...."

"Or, you can let *me* have the sausage." She looked at the tray held so tightly between them. She turned her gaze to his face, looked him directly in the eye. There was a twinkle there, he was almost sure of it. "I'll cook the sausage. You cook the eggs. My place."

Old Jack Fraser finally let go of the sausage and Bob the butcher gave him a wink as they made their way to the checkouts.

*****

Jo-Ann D. MacDonald hails from Cape Breton, NS. She lives with her husband and two sons. When she's not walking her goofy dog, Burger, she is curled up reading a good book.

Nancy Drew inspired her passion for reading and a good mystery. Harry Potter gave rise to her love for fantasy and stirred her desire to write.

Jo-Ann is a member of The Story Forge

writers group. Every November for the past three years, she disappears into her laptop for Nanowrimo (National Novel Writing Month).

Switch

by Kerry A. Campbell

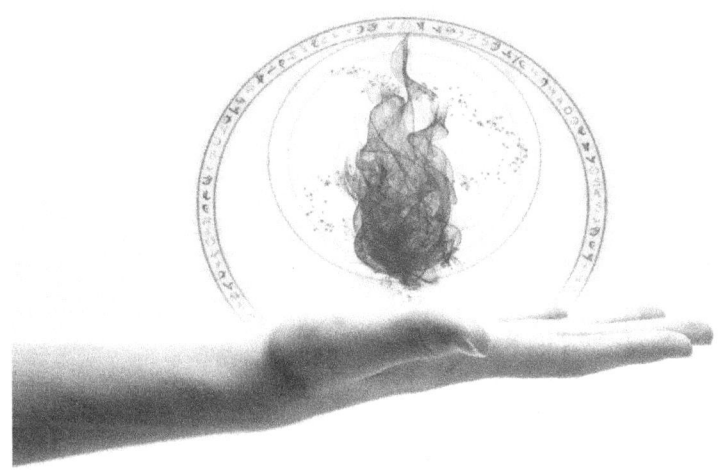

Lily put a tray of mini quiches in the oven. She hoped they would be ready when the first of their guests arrived.

"Who's coming to this thing again?" Quinn asked as he entered the kitchen. He tossed a bag of blood on the counter. It landed with a *plop.*

"Do I wanna know where that came from?" she asked. Sometimes she almost forgot she was dating a vampire.

"Nope, too sinister," he said, and winked at her.

"Eric and his sister are coming," she told him, trying to not think of the bag of blood.

Being a lab tech, she worked with blood, but that was different. At work it wasn't someone's snack. Another bag landed with a sickening *plop.* "They're bringing Duke and Mary, too."

Lily was looking forward to meeting Mary. Eric, Faye and their cousin Duke were werewolves, while Mary was a regular human like herself. Lily was happy she would have another person to talk to about the supernatural world.

"Dimitri texted me a little while ago. He'll be here," Quinn told her.

"Oh, Dimitri is slumming it with us tonight, is he?" she asked, chuckling. Dimitri was a vampire with a taste for the finer things.

"He'd never admit it, but he likes when we all get together," Quinn said.

"I think Eric said Faye was bringing a friend, too. She's a mage. She moved here not long ago and doesn't have many friends," Lily said.

"Well it seems we'll have a nice little crowd," Quinn said. "I hope you got extra appetizers."

"I have six boxes of different ones in the freezer to pop in the oven, plus all the food I've made. A werewolf appetite is a hearty one! Especially Eric's."

Lily admired her work. She had two different dips made in the fridge, a cheeseball and crackers, two meat trays, two fruit trays, plus meatballs in the slow cooker and rice on the stove. Quinn took care of the blood for himself and Dimitri. While vamps ate regular food, it was nice to think of your guests' special diet. Quinn had also picked up beer and wine.

"I think we're all set," Quinn said. "You did an awesome job. Everything smells great."

"Thanks! I hope everyone enjoys it. Finish the the music playlist?"

"Yup. I will go turn it on now."

"Ok. I'll get changed before our guests start arriving."

Lily scooted into her bedroom. A nice evening in was just what she needed. She quickly changed into a pair of light blue jeans and a pink tank top. As she touched up her hair and added a bit of makeup, she could hear Theory of a Deadman's *Bad Girlfriend* start to play.

When Lily emerged from the bedroom, there was a knock on the door.

"I'll get it!" she called out to Quinn.

She headed to the front door, and was greeted by the werewolf pack.

"What smells sooo good?" Eric asked, his nose going into full sniffer mode as he entered the house. Lily heard his stomach growl.

"Lots of good stuff," she told him.

"I hope you prepared for his stomach," Duke said.

"I made enough to feed an army," Lily replied.

"Well that might be enough to feed him," Duke said. The tall red-haired man passed Lily a bag. "Me and Mary picked up a few things. You know, in case he eats everything," he added, giving Lily a wink.

"Hey now, I don't eat that much," Eric protested, feigning being insulted.

Quinn came from down the hallway. "Actually, you do." Quinn clapped his friend's hand, bringing him in for a hug.

"So this is Mary," Duke said, beaming. From what Lily was told, the two had been dating for the last few months.

Lily reached out to hug Mary. "It is so nice to meet you!"

"It's great to meet you, too," Mary said as she hugged Lily back. "I can't exactly tell my friends about...all this," she said, gesturing to the two werewolves and a vampire.

Lily laughed. "Yeah, I know what you mean. We humans gotta stick together," she said. "Come on in, you guys. Where's Faye?"

"Coming in a bit with Emmi," Eric answered, his nose still stuck in the air.

"You guys get comfy in the living room. I'll bring out some snacks. Anyone want a drink?" Lily asked.

Duke and Eric asked for beers. Mary followed Lily into the kitchen to help with the food.

"Is that blood?" Mary asked, spying the red fluid-filled bags.

"Yup," Lily replied as she put the bag Duke gave her on the counter.

"This new world takes getting used to, doesn't it?"

"It does. Luckily we have each other to talk

to. The lone humans in the bunch," Lily replied.

"Thank God I'm not in this alone," Mary said with a little laugh.

"I didn't have anyone to talk to until you," Lily said. "I used to have this one friend, and I told her about the night I saved Quinn. That's how we first met. She thought I was crazy."

"Wait. You saved Quinn?" Mary asked, following Lily back to the living room.

"When a vampire is wrapped up in silver chains, he's like a weak, little baby," Eric said, obviously overhearing the question. "Ow! Dude, you didn't have to hit me," he added, rubbing his hand over his short blond hair.

"Ya, I did," Quinn replied, taking a swig of his beer.

Lily passed Eric a beer. "You're lucky that's all he did."

Mary brought out a bowl of chips and dip as the doorbell rang.

"I'll get it this time." Quinn got up from the sofa and headed to the door.

"Oh crap!" Lily exclaimed. "My quiches!" she ran to the kitchen, hoping not all was lost. She breathed a sigh of relief as she took out the tray.

As she put them on a plate, she heard female voices down the hall.

"Thank God, I thought I burned these," Lily told them as she entered the living room with the food.

"I woulda ate 'em," Eric said.

"I know you would have, my little waste disposal," she replied as their latest guests entered the room.

"You guys, this is Emmi," Faye said.

Emmi smiled. "Thanks so much for having me," she said. She was what Lily pictured a mage would look like. Long, flowy skirt. Looking a bit gypsy-like. Her curly hair seemed to move with a mind of its own.

"Thanks so much for coming," Lily said. "We're happy you could make it."

"What can I get you girls to drink?" Quinn asked. "Beer? Wine? Blood?"

"We'll stick to wine," Faye told him, giving him a wink.

"So, how long have you been practicing magick?" Lily asked Emmi as Quinn went to get two glasses of wine.

"Not that long. My mother and grandmother had the gift. My mother never taught me anything, as she thought it was a curse. My grandmother died when I was four, so she didn't have the chance to teach me."

"That's so sad," Lily said.

Emmi smiled. "Well, I found an old spell book a few years ago in my parents' attic. Apparently, it's been in the family for generations, so I thought maybe I should keep up the family tradition. I started training and learning on my own, about a year and a half ago."

"What brings you to the Cape?" Quinn asked, passing them their drinks.

"There is magic in the ground here, especially in the mountains. I talked to an older witch who lived along the Cabot Trail."

"That's how we met," Faye added. "She found my shop after she moved here. I have been helping her the best I could." Faye loved the occult and owned a shop on the Trail dedicated to it.

The doorbell rang. Lily excused herself and made for the door. Opening it, she was greeted by Dimitri.

"This is for you," Dimitri said formally as he handed her a bottle of her favorite wine.

"Oh, thanks so much." She eyed up his attire. "You are the only one I know who wears a Giorgio Armani suit to a house party," she said as she made room for him to come in.

"Like I would be caught undead wearing jeans and a tee," he replied. "No offense," he added.

Lily rolled her eyes. "None taken. Come on in."

As they walked down into the living room, Dimitri said, "I thought I caught the whiff of dog when I came in."

"What cologne are you wearing, Dimitri? Eau de corpse?" Eric asked.

"Har-de-har-har," Dimitri said, and shook his friend's hand.

The party guests chatted and milled about. Lily made herself busy with bringing food and paper plates out, while Quinn heated two wine glasses of blood for himself and Dimitri.

"You put on quite the spread, Lily," Duke told her as she brought out another tray of food.

"Thanks. I'm impressed with myself. I can feed my guests AND that bottomless pit," she said, as she nodded to Eric, who was eyeing up the meatballs and rice he'd just put on his plate.

Lily was feeling happy and content as she helped serve people and put more appetizers in the oven. The music played her favourite mix under the rumble of voices coming from the living room.

"Need any help?" Quinn asked, as he walked up to her and leaned down for a quick kiss.

"No, I'm good, thanks," she said, smiling up at him.

Eric came into the kitchen. His plate was so clean Lily would almost guess he licked it.

"More meatballs?" she asked him.

The werewolf's green eyes lit up. "Yes please," he said, and she nodded for him to help himself.

Lily grabbed a plate and loaded up on some food for herself. She followed Quinn into the living room and sat next to him. Everyone seemed to be enjoying themselves. Even Dimitri was smiling.

"So, how is the whole magick thing coming, Emmi?" Eric asked her.

"Pretty good, I think," she said.

"Oh, we have a magick user in our midst,

do we?" Dimitri asked, sipping on his glass of blood.

"I'm a mage," Emmi told him. "Well, for just over a year."

"She's been doing great," Faye added. "Come on, show everyone what you've been working on."

Emmi looked flustered. "Nobody wants me to bore them."

"Not boring at all," Lily put in. "I wish I had the ability to use magick."

"Well, okay," Emmi said, sounding more confident.

"Lily, may I borrow this?" Emmi asked, as she picked up a blue stone from the coffee table.

"Sure, it's only something I found on the beach."

Everyone watched as Emmi wrapped her hands around the cool blue stone, closing her eyes as she did so. Even Dimitri watched with interest.

Emmi slowly opened her hands and little blue butterflies fluttered from her palm.

Everyone clapped in awe.

The butterflies fluttered around the room before settling back in Emmi's palm. She closed her hands around them, and when she opened them, there sat the blue stone.

"That is so cool!" Lily exclaimed.

"So awesome!" Duke said.

"Thanks. Just some illusion work," Emmi said, and put the stone back on the table.

"Come on, show us something else," Quinn said.

Emmi reached for her bag and took out a pack of matches. She took one from the pack, struck it on the flint. As the match popped and lit up, Lily watched as Emmi put her fingers over the flame as she plucked it from the match. Emmi 'held' the flame between her thumb and index finger, and transferred it to her palm. The orange ball flickered. Emmi put her other hand over the flame and whispered something. The ball grew. It was now the size of a tennis ball. Lily watched, transfixed, as Emmi played with the ball of flame, moving it from hand to hand, without so much as a flinch.

She put her hands together and a small puff of smoke emerged. The flame was out.

"That is so neat!" Mary exclaimed. "Didn't that hurt you?"

"Not at all. I had complete control. I can feel a bit of warmth, nothing more."

"That is charming," Dimitri drawled. "Can you do anything a bit...bigger?"

"Leave her be," Faye said, sounding annoyed.

"What did I do?" he asked, shrugging.

"Actually, I have something in mind," Emmi said. "Would you like to be part of it?"

"Long as you don't set me on fire, behead me, or put a stake in my heart, sure," he said, and put his bloody wine glass on the table beside him.

"I need another volunteer," Emmi said.

"I'm game!" Eric said.

"Okay, I need you to stand next to each other," Emmi told them.

"Don't give me any of your fleas, Eric," Dimitri said as he stood up.

"Is this something crazy?" Eric asked. "Like, should I be worried here?"

"Oh, not at all. I am just going to change up your wardrobes a bit," she told him.

"Great, I am going to go home smelling like Fido," Dimitri said.

"Ok, just relax," Emmi said, as she closed her eyes.

Lily shifted in her seat. The wine she had earlier was kicking in and she needed to head to the washroom. She stood, intending to zip out of the living room so she wouldn't interrupt the show, but she tripped on Faye's foot. She fell forward as Emmi lifted her hands and began to chant something unintelligible. Lily landed on the floor with a thud as a gust of wind blew over her.

A moment later, Lily opened her eyes. She stared up at the ceiling.

I thought I landed face down.

She heard a male grunt close to her.

Did I knock someone over?

She sat up and looked around. She was on the opposite side of the room.

"What happened?"

She gasped and covered her mouth with her hand. Why did her voice sound so deep? Quinn looked over at her like she had grown extra limbs.

"Sorry, the power of the spell knocked you all over," Emmi said. "Let me help you up, Lily." Just as Lily was about to say no thanks, she watched Emmi reach to someone on the floor.

"I don't need your hand."

My voice!

Lily watched her body sit up.

"What the hell?" she heard her voice ask.

"Christ, why do my clothes feel so...cheap?" she heard Eric ask. Eric looked down at himself. "So much for not being caught undead in jeans and a tee. Hey, why does my voice sound different. Why does-"

Eric looked up and noticed her, eyes widening.

"What did you do, mage?" Eric yelled as he jumped to his feet.

"Whoa whoa, calm down," Quinn said, standing up to get between Emmi and Eric.

"I won't calm down! I am wearing the dog's meatsuit!" Eric yelled.

"What?" Quinn asked.

Emmi gasped.

Eric pointed at Emmi and yelled. "She didn't just change our clothes, Quinn. She switched bodies!"

Quinn looked down at her. "Then Eric is in your body?" he asked.

"Nope," she croaked, and looked down at her hands. Only they weren't her hands anymore. They were Dimitri's large, pale ones.

Laughter broke—her own laughter. Lily's body was cackling. "You're in my body. Now who's the fleabag?"

Lily stood up and made her way to the mirror on the wall.

What she saw was not her own reflection, but indeed Dimitri's. She reached up, touching her cheek. The reflection did the same.

Quinn came up behind her. "Lily?" he asked hesitantly.

"Yup," she responded.

"Oh my God, I am so sorry! This wasn't supposed to happen!" Emmi sobbed, tears welling up in her eyes.

"This is quite the party," Duke said, a wide smile on his face.

"Dudes! I have boobs!" Lily looked over at her body. Eric was making her boobs bounce, smiling as he did so.

"Oh lord, you better not touch those!" Lily shouted.

"You're no fun," Eric said.

"Okay, I think I can fix this!" Emmi seemed to have gotten her emotions under control.

"Maybe you should have your mentor come over and fix this," Dimitri said.

"I-I don't have one," Emmi stuttered. "I've been self-teaching."

Dimitri took in a deep breath but before he could verbally rip into Emmi, Quinn spoke up.

"You're the one who asked her to do something bigger, mister hotshot. You got it."

Dimitri shot Quinn a look of death but said nothing more.

"So what's this idea of yours?" Lily asked.

"Basically a counterspell. Like hitting the *undo* button on a computer," she told them.

As Emmi dug around into her bag, Lily watched Eric walk over to the mirror.

"Are you trying to look at my ass?" Lily asked.

"No," he replied, sheepishly. "Well, maybe just a little. You have a nice butt."

"She does," Dimitri added.

"Stop looking at Lily's butt. Both of you," Quinn said.

Emmi pulled the coffee table closer to her. Lily watched as Emmi put a clam shell on it and took out a little baggie of dirt. She filled the shell and added a few drops of essential oil. Everyone was quiet as Emmi chanted over the shell.

"Okay, the three of you come here," she said. "And hold out your palms."

Emmi took a small bit of dirt from the shell and put in into their outstretched hands. The pack of matches from earlier was still out. Emmi took the pack, lit a match and threw it into the shell.

"Close your eyes," she said. As Lily did, she heard Emmi chanting again.

After several minutes, Emmi said "Okay, open your eyes."

"Did it work?" asked Faye.

"I've still got boobs," Eric said.

Dimitri flung the dirt onto the table.

Emmi's eyes filled and tears rolled down her cheeks. Faye put her arm around her. "It will be okay."

"Easy for you to say," Dimitri said and walked over to her. "You aren't the one stuck in your brother's meatsuit!"

Emmi took a deep breath. "I will fix this, I promise!"

"And I'll help," Faye added.

"Can you do it before sunrise? I don't want princess over there scorching my body by accident," the vampire growled.

"My spell book is out in the car. I'll go get it," Emmi said.

"I'll go with you," Faye told her and the two got up and headed to the front door.

Lily rubbed her ears.

"You okay?" Quinn asked.

"The noise. What's making that thudding sound? There's a lot of it," she said.

"That's the sound of every heartbeat in the room," Dimitri told her.

"How can both of you stand this?" she asked, shaking her head as if trying to get the sound out of it.

"We can tune it out," Quinn told her. "Keep it to a dull roar."

They heard the front door open as the girls came back in.

"You find a spell to fix this?" Dimitri asked.

Faye held up an old, thick book. "It's a three hundred year old book, and there isn't an index. And last I checked there isn't a book called *How to Get A Vampire Out ofAa Werewolf's Body."*

Quinn tried to stifle a laugh but it didn't work.

"Oh shut up. You should be worried about the fleabag in your girlfriend's body."

Lily shook her head. "Enjoying the eyeful?" she asked Eric, who was looking down her top.

"Wha? Oh, sorry," he mumbled. "Quinn's got bigger problems then me," Eric said, looking at Quinn. "His girlfriend is now growing a five o' clock shadow."

Lily put her hand up to her cheek. She could feel the slight bit of stubble growing in. "This is so weird," she muttered.

The skin she touched felt cool. She didn't feel chilly, but she could feel that her body temp was lower then it should be.

"I wish I had some popcorn," Duke said, who was sitting back with his feet on the coffee table, enjoying the show.

"We're going in the kitchen, to look for the spell we need," Faye said.

Dimitri sat on the sofa and crossed his arms.

"These things really dig into ya, don't they?" Eric asked as he tried to shift the bra he was now wearing.

"Least you aren't wearing plaid," Dimitri huffed as he looked down at his overly casual attire.

"I gotta say, Dimitri, you do have great taste

in clothing," Lily said. "Never thought I would look good in a suit."

Mary looked at the switched trio. "And here I was thinking that things couldn't get any weirder then hanging with werewolves and vampires."

"You have no idea," Lily said, sitting in the corner chair. "What's that...smell?" she asked, looking around. "It smells oddly tangy yet sweet."

"That's the blood sitting next to you," Quinn said.

Lily looked over at the wine glass. Some blood remained in the bottom. It didn't turn her stomach. Instead she was tempted to pick it up. Her mouth began to water and suddenly pain hit her as something stabbed her lip.

"Ouch!" Lily exclaimed.

She reached up to touch her lips and felt two fangs.

"Hey, careful with my body!" Dimitri yelled. "I might heal fast, but I want that back in one piece."

Lily noticed the stillness then. The body she inhabited didn't react, aside from the moment of pain from her fangs.

"I...I can't feel a heartbeat," she said.

"And you won't. You're dead as a nit. I forgot what it was like to have a heart beating away at your chest," Dimitri said. "Feels like this thing is gonna explode."

"Hey, it takes a lot to keep that body going," Eric noted.

Lily felt tears well in her eyes.

"Quinn, I don't like this at all," she said, and tears began to run down cool, pale cheeks. She ran over to him and put her arms around him. She felt Quinn wrap his arms around her.

"Oh no, get your hands off him," Dimitri said. "My body in Quinn's arms is not a sight I want to see."

"I feel like I'm about to watch male-on-male vamp porn," Eric added.

"Would you two shut up? Lily didn't exactly expect to be a vampire today. You can't prepare for that shit," Quinn said.

"I gotta pee," Eric said, and got up.

"Oh no you don't!" Lily said. "Hold it in!"

"Why?"

"It's one thing for you to check out my girlfriend's chest," Quinn started. "But keep your paws off her lady bits."

"Son of a bitch," Eric said with a sigh as he sat back down. "I forgot I'm missing my best feature."

"That's the least of your worries," Dimitri said. "I don't know what's worse. Being Eric or a human."

"There's nothing wrong with being human," Mary said. "Although I am kinda jealous of what some of you can do."

"Oh my God," Eric said, crossing his legs. "Like, I really gotta pee."

"Sorry. I was heading to the washroom when I fell," Lily told him.

Emmi came bursting out of the kitchen.

"We might have a solution!"

"What is it?" Dimitri and Lily asked at the same time.

"I called a friend of mine," Faye began. "We think Emmi mispronounced one of the words in her incantation. So instead of switching clothes, you switched bodies."

"Switching you back will need a different spell. If I did the same one, you will switch again but might not end up in the right body," Emmi explained.

"So what is this solution you mentioned?" Dimitri asked.

"I will need the three of you to stand in a circle, and hold hands," Emmi began. "Then, as I say the incantation, focus on your body, and imagine you are floating back into it."

"Do we say this spell along with you?" Lily asked.

"No, just focus on your body along with these words: *body mine, body thine, let my body and soul entwine.*"

"But I don't have a soul," Dimitri said.

"You don't know that. Besides, you have an essence."

Lily, Dimitri and Eric moved to the middle of the living room. They held hands as they had been instructed.

Emmi took three candles out of her bag.

"What don't you have in there?" Duke asked.

"I never leave home with out my bag," she told him.

She put a candle in front of Lily, Eric and Dimitri and with a flick of a wrist they were lit.

"Okay, close your eyes, focus on your body and think of the chant I gave you," Emmi instructed.

Lily did as she was told. She pictured being in her own body. The warmth, the heart beat in her chest. She began to feel lighter, as if she was floating. *Body mine, body thine, let my body and soul entwine. Body mine, body thine, let my body and soul entwine.* As she inwardly repeated the chant, she heard the faint murmuring of Emmi performing the spell.

She felt a movement of air swirl around her as everything went silent. Lily held her breath. She didn't budge. She was too afraid to move.

Did it work?

"Okay everyone, open your eyes," Emmi said.

Lily slowly opened one eye and looked to her right. There was Eric, looking down at himself. She opened the other eye and–

"Oh yes!" Dimitri shouted. He let go of their hands and began to give himself a pat down.

Lily looked at the mirror hanging on the wall. She smiled. Her reflection did the same.

She was giddy with relief as she ran into Quinn's arms.

"Either I got my girlfriend back or Eric has been dying to kiss me," Quinn said as Lily kissed his cheek.

"In your dreams, bloodsucker," Eric said.

"Oh no!" Lily exclaimed. "I gotta pee!" and

she dashed off.

When Lily came out of the washroom, she noticed Emmi and Faye walking towards the front door.

"Hey, where are you two going?" she asked. "There's still lots of food left."

Emmi looked over at her, barely looking her in the eye. "I think it's best I go. I'm sorry about everything, Lily."

"Wait," Eric said, coming up behind Lily. "You should stay."

"After the problem I caused?"

Dimitri crossed the room to stand next to Eric. "You also fixed it. Next time you want to put a vamp in a werewolf body, do it to Quinn, would you?"

Emmi chuckled. "Yeah, sure."

"We've all been through much worse then this," Lily said.

"Okay, I'll stay if Faye is up for it," Emmi said, smiling.

Eric's stomach growled. "Feels like I haven't eaten in ages," he said, and made his way to the kitchen.

"Well," Quinn said, as the room began to buzz with chatter once again. "How did you like being a vampire?"

"I think I will stick to my human form," she told him.

"Want a drink?" Quinn asked as he held up a wine glass, blood pooling at the bottom.

"Oh God, no!"

"Well, it's good to have things back to

normal," he said.

"Or as normal as they get around here," she said, as she looked around the room at her not-so-normal friends.

*****

Kerry Anne Campbell lives in Cape Breton with her husband, feisty yet lovable cat, and rescue greyhound. When not engrossed in a good book or deep in one of her own made-up worlds, she can be found sipping iced coffees, going to comic con or painting nails for a living.

She loves to ramble on her blog over at thegeekybooklady.wordpress.com and pin loads of fun things on Pinterest (find her at https://www.pinterest.ca/kerryanne82/). So far she has four short stories published with Third Person Press in their *Elements* series, and hopes to publish a novel when she learns to stop procrastinating.

Snack Raps

by Kyle MacNeil

Ickles

Bumpy Slimy
Lumpy Grimy
Ick!
Pickles make me sick
Your emerald sheen
is the foulest green
the world has ever seen
You're awful when you're sour
you're worse when you're sweet
your bread and butter tastes like feet
but know I won't be beat
If I get you on my break
I'm taking you back

You won't sully my Big Mac
I hate the smell when I'm workin'
It's always lurkin'
I'm IRKED BY GHERKINS!
They hold highest office on my shit-list
I've never seen a dumber plant
than this cucumber incumb-er-ent
Their salty juice
is like a noose on my tongue
they taste like dung!
And I'd rather be hung
then bite a crunchy dill
I've had my fill
it's over
I don't care if it's kosher
These veggies are a crime
I won't say *L'chaim*
Either they're gone, or I am
I don't mean to be a spastic
but I see nothing classic
about a Vlasic
And god help ye
If you give any other veggies a vinegar bath
You've incurred my wrath
You psychopath
If you like your cukes fermented
you're demented
My opinion is cemented
buried in the pavement is where these freaks
are meant to be
It's either them or me
Pickles are my worst enemy.

My Secret Shame

My secret shame
It's pervasive
Abrasive
I hate it
Do they know when I come off break?
Are they aware of what I ate
When I sneak in,
Grease on my lips
Rub my fingers on my hips
Big red cup
sneaking sips
The more I conceal
The more I reveal
That something is up
They all stare at my big red Wendy's cup
I love their beef
Always fresh, never icy
Their chicken burgers are actually spicy
But things are getting dicey
I think I'm in trouble
I don't care
I love the Dave's double
and I'm ready to mingle
With the Dave's single
Don't get me started on those chicken strips
When those chicken bits
hit my traitor lips
I'm in traitorous bliss
And the Frosties?
Please

I'm on my knees
God damn I love Wendy's.

***

Hamburglar

I'm the next
in a long line of
sandwich thieves
I'm the hamburglar
Please
Don't tell Mayor McCheese
Sometimes
they just made extras
sometimes they're off a tray
so I sneak in
awfully dexterous
and take a McDouble away
but I won't touch your
Fish Filet
or your "chicken"
it's dirty
it's made from my friend Birdie
When I see a Junior
I just want to hug it
Because they fried my little nugget
so yeah
I have a beef with the chief
Who's made me frown chronically
He's a clown ironically
sitting on a throne of fries
all Ronald McDonaldly
He's pushed me to my limits

and now my frowns
become a Grimace
Give me space
I'm turning purple in the face
And its looking like these burgers
are catching up to my waist
I'm a beast
But one that's been long pestered
by that jolly ginger jester
It may be childish
but his words are lost on me
I'm a violent violet Monstrosity
Snap
I've torn the clown in half
now who has the last laugh
we're free
Rotten Ronnie's been socked
his reign is over
he's been Shamrocked
like a shake made of clover
I take a seat
Its time to chow
someone grind up a cow
I'm the Burger King now.

***

Upsell

Upsell! Upsell!
Upsell your soul to me
Your soul was sold to me
For a side of fries
This soul, This soul

This soul will toll for me
Working on patrol for me
Until the day he dies
This toll, This toll
This toll is killing me
It's not fulfilling, see
working 9-5
Black out, Black out
My chest feels like a thunderstorm
So why'm I in my uniform
Am I still alive?
No sir, No sir
This window's not for living folk
This hell isn't some sort of joke
It seems your brain's deep fried.
My god, My god
How long have I been working here
It's like it's been a hundred years
Please sir I'm terrified
1 year, 100 years
1000 years you've worked for me
You'll work here for eternity
We hunger for your cries
Ronald, Ray Kroc
You bastards and the rest of ye
You'll never get the best of me
Even if you try
You'll see, You'll see
As sure as diet soda's wet
I'll file my 2 weeks' notice yet
So try that on for size
Drive thru, Drive thru,
Window

Of Opportunity
Jump on out and now I'm free
End my shift, open my eyes
I'm free, I'm free
I've escaped this burger hell
I've no more need to upsell
You bastards on some fries

***

Chilly Days

The Blistering Cold
Canadian Climate
Does no favors for
this Primate
The wind alone is
chill inducent
Goose pimpled skin
near translucent
I thirst for the sun
but all is cloud
Yet here you bellow
Rather loud
4 McFlurries
Add hot fudge
While your tires
swim through sludge
You approach
my window sill
yet I don't
open my till
As the frostbite
slowly trickles

you sort trough
a fist of nickels
When I clutch your
frozen cash
Your tires squeal
and with a splash
You drive ahead
Rather rude
and grab your frozen
dairy food
I close the window
and hope it'll stay
to warm up on
this stormy day
PS I find it
rather scary
you bought ice cream
in January

***

Bagel Guy

Bagel guy,
hater, not a waiter
you make me,
my coworkers
and probably yours cry
Sitting up there on your pedestal
Your too-tall truck,
foot on the pedal
Still Screaming at me
Why?
Because I didn't catch your coffee

Snack Raps

And you ask for something edible?
Sorry to say
but your food will be delayed
yet you force it down your gullet
could be worse
you could swear and curse
or sport a mullet
But you're a man of the law
and your hair's all trimmed
those books they made you read
public relations; your flaw
I assume they were skimmed?
I don't mean to be the quarreler
but when we take your order
we need to know more sir
We can't read minds
we know you're not blind
when you order a #5
A gentleness in your voice
when you make your choice
it goes a long way
And you'll be caught dead
before you pull ahead
so take your food asshole
and have a nice day.

***

McCafe Haikus

Cappuccino Dreams
Foam pearls in a Dairy Sea
Keeps ya up all night

Coffee lid sideways
Joe scalds my extremities
Incident Report

Large Double-Double
Want to pair that with Cookies?
2 for 1 special

Dollar Coffee Days
Come here while Tim Horton's is
Rolling up the Rim

Lattes and Mochas
Only diff is chocolate
Now you know the truth

Earl Grey, the best tea
Rarely sold, but always bold
Love that Froot Loops taste

Free coffee coupon
7th cup is free
40 cent upcharge

Americanos
Slightly better than coffee
Espresso Water

Screaming in the mic
Wait your turn lady, Jesus
The worst customers.

***

In loving memory of McDonalds Mom

Like a true captain
you kept us afloat
you ran a tight ship
When I was fresh off the boat
With I as your swabbie
and Jay your first mate
you made any 6am
morning shift great
You paced back and forth
starboard to port
When you were on deck
Our supplies weren't short
You fixed every problem
When you were the driver
Like a four foot, redhead
Mcdonalds MacGyver
And even if facing
a mutinous crew
I'd walk the plank
before I'd betray you
From advice about life
to repairing the soda
You're wise for your size
Like a morning-shift Yoda
You kept us from getting

Too overwhelmed
It won't be the same
without you at the helm
It may be a long time
Till I next see my friend
But the SS Diana
Will set sail again

*****

Kyle Mac Neil is a relatively new writer whose attention can rarely be kept on one project at a time but is pleased to finally finish one. He has written poetry for North Poets and is currently writing a fantasy novel, though writer's block hasn't been doing him any favors. He also produces video content on YouTube at the Dr. Whippersnatch channel.

He considers himself the freshest thing to come out of a McDonalds, and hopes you enjoy his Snack Raps, a collection of poetry he wrote when he should have been working.

His section of the anthology is dedicated to his late friend Diana.

The Slick Pastor Flax

by Devin J. Meaney

His sermon was just coming to a close as the slick Pastor Flax purged the sugar demons from one of his faithful followers. "I cleanse you from this man, sugared menace!" shrieked the Pastor as he did his work. The man screamed with joy as the entities fled from him, his mind now filled with visions of raw carrot sticks and no-dip cauliflower.

Never again would the man eat pastries. No cake or refined sugar of any sort would disgrace his life. The Pastor had shown him the way of the flax. Sugar demons hated anyone who lived a healthy lifestyle, leaving soon after the first bite of flax, the nutritious demon-fighting wonder food.

His faithful were taken care of for the day, but the slick Pastor knew that tomorrow would bring on more work that needed to be done."What more can I do? What can I do to be better? How can I help create a better world?" he muttered under his breath as he prepared to end his day.

His life revolved around the flax and its wonderful anti-demonic properties. Every day he fought against a scourge of cola chains, fast food franchises and the rising belt-size of the average Canadian. Everywhere he looked, the flax was needed. Nothing would stop him on his rise to fame as he released sugar demons left and right, his mind reciting prophecy he had read within the writings of Richard Simminz, his hero.

Simminz knew all about the sugar demons, his teachings key to the slick Pastor's preaching. Slick Pastor Flax had originally heard of Simminz back in his college days, when he did work-outs at the local yoga center. To this day he follows this guru in his works relentlessly, toiling himself half to death as he spreads the word of the flax. Simminz never responded to any of the Pastor's emails, but if he knew of the good that was being done, the slick Pastor was sure that Simminz would be proud of him.

Right before bed, he sent one last email to Simminz, feeling that the guru's input was crucial to his work. "Please answer me, oh great one, I need your guidance and divine light!" he prayed one last time before he slowly drifted off to sleep.

The next day, while the Pastor recited the preachings of Richard Simminz to his faithful, an unfamiliar man walked into the Pastor's church. He was known throughout the town as Grumpy Lumpy, a man almost everyone knew was keen to the sugar. He was not a pleasant man to be around, as the sugar demons had consumed his life. He ate donuts for breakfast and donut holes for lunch. For supper he drank whipped cream from the carton, his eyes bulging from his head as the sugar demons took hold.

The townies had no sympathy for him, but Pastor Flax knew that this was just a man that needed help. He was only lumpy because of his excessive sugar intake. With help from the words of his hero Simminz, the Pastor knew he could make a change in this man's life.

"Come here, my son," said the pastor in a tone riddled with empathy.

Lumpy walked up to Flax's altar, pure sugar pouring from his ears as he made his way to the Pastor. Pure fructose streamed from his eyes as he tearfully told the slick Pastor of his plight.

"I had a relapse! I was trying to eat healthier, but after a while I just couldn't take it anymore! I ate three cartons of ice cream, four pies and an entire pound of granulated sugar. This released an army of sugar demons

97

from the back of my brain and now I do not know how to get rid of them!"

Pastor Flax cracked his knuckles as he prepared to do his work. He had seen this before–but never this extreme. It would take all of his will power and accumulated knowledge to do this. He even doubled up on Lumpy's first dose of flax as a way to fight the demons that scurried about in the man's addled brain.

Beginning his work, Pastor Flax recited passages from the many books Simminz had released, posing in yoga stances as he desperately tried to help Lumpy. He intoned many different chants and mantras but it seemed as if nothing was going to work. The sugar demons were clearly deeply ingrained within Lumpy's mind and it seemed it would take a force of extreme nature to cure his sugary affliction.

"It's as if his diet consisted solely of twinkies and cream soda since his birth!" concluded the Pastor under his breath.

Just then, after the Pastor finished reciting his last mantra, Lumpy began to vibrate. His eyes rolled into the back of his head and he started speaking in a voice that was not his. This was no longer Lumpy.

Pastor Flax paled. He feared he might recognize the entity–the demonic sugar pseudo-god the legions of the underworld called Dark Cookies.

"ANYONE WANT A COOKIE?" the demon yelled grotesquely from Lumpy's contorted face. The demon chortled. "I've come to take this man back to hell with me as my slave! He has consumed more sugar than your entire town! He must be forsaken to frolic in misery within the abysmal void, a land where there exists nothing but sugar!"

Pastor Flax felt panic churn his stomach. Lumpy's head spun, like in that movie where the girl throws up pea soup. It was not pea soup Lumpy was vomiting though; he spewed cream soda, his projectile sprays coating the church like a demonic soda pop fountain. Lumpy screamed in tongues as he blasphemed against the teachings of Richard Simminz, his mind and voice now obviously under the complete control of Dark Cookies.

The slick Pastor needed a miracle, and he needed it quick. It seemed as if the church itself would implode, the aisles now riddled with relentless demonic activity.

At that moment, a cloaked figure walked elegantly through the front doors of the church. Whoever it was, the sugar demons seemed to sense them and their activity increased. The cloaked figure made its way to Lumpy and the Pastor, its cape trailing as it approached Flax's altar. The figure removed its hood. The slick Pastor gasped as his heart jumped.

"It's Richard Simminz himself!" cooed the Pastor. "He must be here to save the day and stop Dark Cookies in his tracks!"

"Someone email for a spiritual

intervention?" asked Simminz casually as his eyes glinted with the knowledge of the universe.

Simminz had not answered the Pastor's previous emails, but Flax somehow understood that the guru's keen senses had made him choose the perfect time to appear. He had probably picked up on the dark forces lurking within the aura of the small town even before he made it to the church, and knew things were grave.

Pastor Flax nodded, telling Simminz that he clearly could not handle this all on his own and Dark Cookies needed to be stopped.

Simminz screamed as he summoned the forces of the Flax Gods. Pastor Flax gasped. The divine power of the Gods themselves would be needed to stop this looming scourge?

Pastor Flax watched in awe as Simminz chanted his most powerful mantras, his temples pulsing as he tried to send the demons back from wence they came. The Flax Gods sent him all of their power, and his biceps bulged as his body consumed the godly energy. The fight was going well, but Dark Cookies was still in control of Lumpy.

"YOU CANNOT STOP THE DARK GOD OF COOKIES!" the pseudo-god screamed as he held on to Lumpy.

The Gods themselves were having trouble purifying him, his essence reeking of desperation, hatred and empty calories. The Pastor jumped in and began to chant along with Simminz. The guru was a force to be reckoned with, but the Pastor himself was no amateur.

"Let's see how you handle the both of us, you high calorie bastard!" he screamed as he got ready to face the dark pseudo-god. His mantras and yogo stances were vital to the cleansing of the church and the tides of battle quickly began to change.

The people still in the pews also started chanting, and with the addition of more voices, the church filled with a light of hope. The battle lasted half an hour, but in the end Dark Cookies went scurrying back to hell, his minions never to bother Lumpy again.

Lumpy promised to never again binge on sugars, and to this day his diet is filled with vegetables, whole grains, flax and assorted fruits. Never again would he let the demons take hold, his life now purified.

"Thank you my friends, I will never forget this," said Lumpy sheepishly but sincerely. Lumpy was soon loved by the town as his whole persona was now changed. He would spend the rest of his days fighting the sugar demons with slick Pastor Flax and his congregation, his heart now filled with love and joy.

Simminz also decided to stay and help Pastor Flax as he thought his presence was needed. Working together, Lumpy, the slick Pastor Flax, Simminz and the congregation would eventually wipe out all demonic sugar activity in town, turning the whole place into a paradise the Flax Gods themselves would be proud of.

The battle was still waged daily in other parts of the world, but for now, we will end with a happily ever after, at least knowing that Lumpy is safe. The sugar demons would never again plague the town, the paradise standing strong until the end of time. Everything was perfect, flax and carrot sticks with no-dip cauliflower readily available for all in the land.

George: A Tale of Feathers and Fun

by Devin J. Meaney

Dedicated to Uncle Kevin

In my younger years, I enjoyed spending time at my grandparents' home. My uncle told me dramatic and in-depth tales filled with adventure. One of these tales was of George, the giant chicken. He was my uncle's best friend, and apparently, he was pretty popular with the ladies. I never saw him, as he was afraid and shy around children. I knew he was real, though; he would always steal coffee and other goodies from the cabinets and drawers in my grandparents' kitchen.

Sometimes, I would find large feathers in the backyard...George was afoot, I knew it! I knew he was around, because he was friends with the giant mouse in the basement whom I knew was not a character from fiction. If the mouse was real, what was so strange about George? I saw the mouse once, and I pray to never see him again, but I craved seeing George. I would perform poorly-planned stake-outs to try to catch a glimpse of the elusive chicken. I hunted George like a cat hunts a sparrow, but sadly, the chicken was never found.

Years passed and I never stopped looking for George. Well on into my teens I would still search for him, his presence always evading my prying eyes. Even now as an adult, I sometimes wonder... when I am alone at night and I can feel unseen eyes burning into the back of my skull—is it George? After all these years...has the chicken stuck around? I really don't know. What I do know, is that a story told by my uncle has inspired years of detective work and a love for an unseen poultry-shadow that has escaped capture for nearly three decades, maybe more. I realize now that George MAY have been a rooster, but as it is now 2018 I think it is safe to say George can be whatever he wants to be.

George the chicken was, and still is, a family classic, and to this day, I am still finding footprints in the backyard. I can put two and two together as I write this and conclude that George is probably alive and well. If not, he will forever be in my heart and dreams, his tale inspiring many stories... including this one. George is legend, his tale now finally scrawled in pen and ink, never to be forgotten by those who loved him and many others. Will it draw him from hiding? Who knows? Maybe someday I will see him, but for now I will settle with this quick narration, a tale of wonder, and the giant 'chicken' from the Mines.

*****

Devin Joseph Meaney is the beloved author of many reviews and shorts that nobody actually reads. Within the nine hundred years he has been on this planet, he has been a cart boy, a scrap metal dude, a traffic control technician and was twice the world's coolest dishwasher. He spent a brief period in online marketing, but found that selling coma-inducing sugared beverages to pre-teens was not his style. He has a beautiful young daughter whom he loves very much, his cat Simba being the commander and chief/C.E.O of his many plots and various schemes.

Devin is also a goregrind/grindcore musician who has put out many demos, ep's and albums, even though he has not picked up the guitar professionally since 2013. He would like to thank his writers group for continued support, Dave Wolff from Autoerotic-asphyxium Zine, and a big thank you also going to Betty Rocksteady and James Buick for giving him the inspiration to pick up a pen and paper in the beginning.

Gram and Gramp

by Roberta Fraser

Gram

My earliest memory of my mother's mother, born Annie Ryan, is from my crib, sick with a cold or flu; Gram came into our room and held a steaming cup of hot tea with lemon to my lips, encouraging me to drink and I would feel better. It must have worked, because I remember the incident and have become an avid tea drinker beginning with two cups for breakfast. A good cup of tea has been a 'comfort' drink all my life.

It must have been Gram who gave me a good memory for some banal events of no importance to anyone except the doer and the witnesses to childhood achievements or hurts.

"Remember when you got poison ivy when you were walking to school in Grade One?" she asked me when I was adult. Of course I remember the horrible itching and running sores, but it seems strange that she recalls what happened to me. Gram was always very concerned for my welfare and did all she could to make me happy or cure what ailed me.

I was a tomboy who loved the outdoors; my friends and I played in the sandbox when we were four and five, played at Cowboys and Indians when we were six or seven; after those years we hiked, swam, skated and sledded and gardened and rode bicycles and played baseball or badminton. Aside from the cowboy boots, vest, and hat, blue jeans and tee shirts were my uniform and my brown leather paratrooper boots were prized. My mother never bought me any of those clothes that I loved; Gram and Gramp did. Sometimes the Easter bunny brought a new pair of blue jeans.

The wringer washer was in the basement of our house; under the stairs, hanging on a nail, was the rag bag where my mother placed clothing that was torn or worn out or blue jeans which she did not wish me to wear. In her mind little girls should wear lacy, frilly dresses while roaming the woods and fields and climbing trees and hacking out a vegetable garden in the back yard.

On Sundays when Gram and Gramp visited, I would run down the stairs and take my blue jeans needing a knee patch out of the rag bag, and slip them to Gram. She always carried a large cloth bag with wooden handles which was a shopping bag doubling as a purse. Gram slipped the blue jeans into the depths of her bag. She patched the knees with a double piece of cloth hand stitched all around the outside of each patch as well as tiny stitches all around the hole; Gram did not own a sewing machine. The next Sunday she returned my good as new jeans when Mom wasn't looking.

When I think of the fact that many times Gram patched my jeans in defiance of her daughter's wishes, I wonder how she got away with it with never an angry word overheard by me. Gram understood my love for the outdoors and the fact that jeans were very practical in my case. You don't slide down haystacks with a dress on.

Gram was the best reuser I knew; she saved the string the butcher wrapped around the brown paper which contained the meat she bought, the paper bags her groceries were packed in, and buttons and hooks from clothes which had reached the rag bag. She also saved green stamps which were a bonus from the grocery store. These she pasted into a booklet and redeemed for merchandise when her book or books were full. Gram obtained most of her towels, sheets and pillowcases with books of green stamps. Gramp tied the thick white string onto kites which we flew on windy days; he also laid out the rows of his garden with it or encouraged beans to climb it.

Gram always said something nice about people she encountered; I never heard her make a negative comment about anyone. She was a better person than I am in that respect. She always said she was going to live to be one hundred; she wrote that comment in a letter to me after she had been ill. "I'll fool them all," she wrote, "I'll live to a hundred." And she did. Her attitude towards life gave me food for thought; how much of what we believe can or will come true?

Gram certainly influenced me and shaped my personality and attitudes in positive ways. Most of all Gram always cooked Thanksgiving dinner and mince, pumpkin and apple pies, and Easter dinner with ham and the same pies. Gram taught me to enjoy simple pleasures and the pleasures of cooking and doing for others. She taught me to allow my children to grow in their own ways without my restrictions except to protect their safety. Gram allowed me to be me when I was a child.

I recall picking a dandelion one day when my granddaughter was about two years old. I picked it and lifted it under my nose and breathed in audibly so she would get the idea of smelling a flower. She picked a dandelion and imitated me, sniffing loudly. Since then we have picked more aromatic flowers and enjoyed their unique scents. I have watched her as she is growing; the first thing she does after she picks a flower is lift it to her nose and inhale its scent. She is enjoying one of the simple pleasures in life, thanks to great-great-grandparents she never knew–but maybe she does in a way. I smile in fond remembrance.

Gramp

My grandfather, Howard Malcolm Blaydes, known to me as Gramp, was the oldest son and firstborn child in America to emigrants from Yorkshire, England. He went to school through Grade Eight, but soon after that his father was injured at work in a foundry and a few weeks later died from his injuries. Gramp, fourteen years old, was offered a job at the foundry which he took, as no social security or death benefits existed at that time. He supported his mother and five siblings.

When I was four years old, Gramp and Gram were driving to Rhode Island to visit relatives; Gramp hit the bridge over a railway track. He had taken a stroke; the doctor told him he would never walk again. So Gram and Gramp moved in with us. What a fortunate child I was! Gramp would read endless stories from my mother's old school books. Gramp also allowed me to learn words by myself. He was a patient man. When he read a word, I tried to find it on the page. Thus it was that I came to understand what reading was about and could read some simple words before going to school. We spent many happy hours on the sofa that winter, reading together.

Gramp was also trying to walk again; he

was stubborn. He fell against the walls of the hallway many times but made continuous progress. By the next spring he felt well enough to apply for a job selling Ditto machines; selling became his new occupation and was not as strenuous as other jobs. Gram and Gramp moved out before I began school. I missed his companionship and our reading sessions.

Gram and Gramp never owned a house; Gramp always tried to rent a place with space for a garden. He always had a large vegetable garden to provide food for his widowed mother and five siblings. When I was seven they rented the second floor of a house with a large back yard and room for a large garden; there was also a shed for tools. We had moved into rooms in the house next door while our new house was being built.

Gramp had planted a garden and one day I found him there pulling weeds by hand. Of course I wanted to help. Gramp showed me how the emerging seeds were planted in rows and what some of the vegetables looked like at that stage. He patiently explained that I should pull out anything that looked like grass and did not look like a two or four leaf seedling in a straight line. Gramp worked on one row and I worked on an adjacent one, sometimes asking him to tell me if this or that green plant was weed or vegetable.

Then we both finished our rows and I started on another row which was filled with one inch high green grass. I pulled out the grass faithfully, not missing a blade. Gramp finished his second row and came over where I was working.

"Oh, Pet. Those were blades of corn just coming up, not grass."

I felt very badly and my face must have shown it. Gramp said he had a half package of corn in the shed. We found it and we planted more corn in the same row that I had "weeded out." Gramp said, "If you never make a mistake, you never learn." I have learned a lot over the years.

Gramp knew what was important in life; hard work, reading, companionship, stubborness, learning from mistakes, and unlimited love for Pet.

***

Special Delivery

by Roberta Fraser

Ladies, think twice if you consider marrying a farmer. I will tell you the story of Sue; her meeting with her farmer, her engagement, wedding, reception, and deliveries of two sons. If this narrative does not convince you to be wary of marrying a farmer, I don't know what will.

Sue had good friends who worked with her. One lady and her husband used to take Sue to her old home on Sundays to visit her elderly parents. The lady sent Sue down the road a bit to a farm to buy fresh eggs to bring back home–several dozen for her friends who loved farm

114

fresh eggs.

Sue was sent to the hen barn to purchase the eggs, where three brothers were grading eggs. She introduced herself; they probably had heard of her via the grapevine because she had previously visited her friends' parents. Sue was introduced to Sam, Joe and Ernie. All the time they talked to Sue, they continued to candle and grade eggs, close the dozen cartons and place them in fifteen dozen egg boxes.

Sue watched, fascinated by the fast-moving hands grabbing the eggs which tumbled gently off the grader, tipped off by weight into sections for extra large, large, medium and small. The brother who cartoned up the eggs had stacks of large and medium cartons on the table in front of the appropriate size eggs tumbling from the grader. Joe filled a dozen eggs in four motions holding three eggs in each of his large hands. Extra large and large went into the large cartons, so the customer got a good deal. There were not many medium eggs and rarely a small one.

The oldest brother, Sam, candled the eggs and put aside any with blood in them or a very rough shell. These eggs went to the house for baking. The youngest brother, Ernie, lifted the baskets of eggs to a platform at the beginning of the grader and placed eggs on the dual conveyor. At the end of grading he taped the fifteen dozen boxes shut and placed them against the wall.

It was Joe who became most interested in

Sue. Sam made his opinion very clear to anyone who would listen. He had enough troubles without marrying. Later, when Sue would visit on Sunday afternoons, Joe let Sue place the eggs in cartons. [Wife test number one passed successfully; Sue could do his grading job quite competently.]

Spring came, and with it lots of lambs, born in the old sheep barn with its tacked-on fenced enclosure. Joe took care of the sheep and lambs. He built small pens to hold an individual ewe and her lamb or lambs. The lambs were very cute; at three or so weeks of age they would leap into the air throughout the barn and out into the yard on fine days. Sue soon learned how to feed the hay and grain, fill water buckets and help slice mangels (a type of beet) into the yard as a treat.

Sue was not very good at handling the large knife and chopping slices off a large mangel tucked under one's arm. Joe was expert at it. However, Sue was better than Joe at one thing; she could get her smaller hands into a ewe who was straining at lambing. Eventually Sue became the midwife for the flock. [Sue liked sheep and could do most of the work. I think Sue should have ceased buying eggs every Sunday afternoon, but she didn't.]

Summer came, and with it, haymaking. Sue had learned to drive on a tractor with her friend at ten years of age. She didn't know how to hook up machines, but she learned enough that first summer of visiting to be useful tedding or raking the hay. Joe was quite glad to hook up the tedder as long as Sue would drive for hours. Sue also drove the wagon while the brothers loaded the bales of hay, Joe always making the load. [Joe understood that Sue liked to work outdoors and was a competent driver.]

Fall and winter came, and visits to the country were not as frequent. The gravel road was notoriously slippery with thick ice most of the winter. Rain or freezing rain made the road going-into-the-ditch slippery. However, Joe wrote letters and Sue replied. Once or twice they met in Sydney and took in a movie. [Watch out, Sue; Joe wants a relationship that doesn't cost much money.]

The next spring Sue came to visit and helped with the lambs. She was still buying eggs for her friend. Once the sheep and lambs were put out on pasture except for a few ewes who lambed late in April, Joe asked Sue, in the sheep barn, to marry him. Sue said she would. [No engagement ring, ever.]

Sue and Joe had to set a date. Joe insisted it must be after all the hay was baled and packed into the barns. They went to the minister who said he could marry them on short notice if the ceremony was in the manse. That was okay with Sue as she did not go to any church. So the wedding happened one day in mid August after the haying was finished. They took the van which delivered eggs and went to Dartmouth to order a package cedar house, but only the beams and the plans. A stone buried itself in the radiator outside of Truro on the way up. A very nice young mechanic in Bible Hill repaired the leak and did not charge very much when he learned they were on their honeymoon–all three days of it.

Sue and Joe arrived back at the farm and hired a man to dig the basement of their house. The foundation was poured. Laminated cedar beams were inserted into pockets in the rear wall; in the front the beams projected out of pockets ten feet and were the support for a deck which would span the front of the house. All they did that fall was roof over the basement and put tar paper down. After the wedding in August Sue and Joe had the wedding reception in October. Sue's family did not arrive until the day after the reception because their flight was cancelled due to thunderstorms in the airport area. Otherwise it was a good dinner with friends and some of Joe's family.

So Sue and Joe had a basement, no well water, a septic system that worked if you poured a bucket of water hauled from the barn into it, a furnace that worked, and a chimney. They lived in the basement for two years. They had a bed, stove, fridge, two aluminum beach chairs and two pet lambs, Greedy Guts and Bonehead.

Greedy Guts was a tiny black lamb. After a poor start in life with a mother who only had enough milk for one lamb, Greedy Guts was fed with a bottle in the basement. There she thrived and soon jumped into laps when Sue and Joe sat in the aluminum chairs. She nuzzled all around their faces and occasionally nipped an ear. When she was hungry she did not hesitate to bump their calves or bite their fingers, reminding them to get the bottle of milk warmed up. Greedy Guts obviously thought she was a people and needed an ovine companion in the worst way.

Bonehead was brought in from the barn because he was so big and awkward. The large white ram lamb may have been suffering from a lack of selenium. Injections of selenium and vitamins cured him. Joe's father told him that pet lambs would never breed. He was wrong about that, however. Greedy Guts produced many small black lambs for several years. She would come to Sue and Joe in the pasture or if she was in the barn awaiting the birth of her lambs and bump their thighs. She knew them and they knew her.

Greedy Guts was eight years old when she had her last lambs one Sunday morning when Joe was in church. Sue found her south of the sheep barn, which had a one foot thick pack of ice in front. She had dropped one black lamb on the ice and was licking it off. Sue picked up the lamb and Greedy Guts reluctantly followed into the barn, where Sue placed fresh hay on the floor. Greedy Guts produced two more tiny black lambs soon after. She ended her career with triplets but couldn't feed them all. Sue and Joe now placed orphan lambs into a separate pen and fed them bottles.

During the summer of the second year, Sue and Joe hired carpenters to put the main floor on the basement. They moved upstairs in the first week of August; Sue was quite pregnant carrying dishes and bedclothes and clothing upstairs. One day Sue was unloading bales from a wagon, turning half way around, and placing the bale on a conveyor which carried it up into the hay loft of the one hundred year old barn where Joe was packing. Sue was feeling a bit wet, so went into the farmhouse and told Joe's mother. She told Sue to stop lifting bales because it would not be long until labour began.

A couple of days later labour pains came sporadically. Sue told Joe when he came in for his second breakfast after milking the cows. Joe told Sue he couldn't take her to the hospital yet; he had to change the oil and filter on the old gray Ford tractor. Could Sue wait until after dinner at noon? Sue did not feel like eating but fed Joe. Joe took a shower and he and Sue set off down the unpaved gravel full of potholes and washboard ridges at top speed. Every bump caused Sue more pain and she finally told Joe to slow down. Joe was more excited or nervous than Sue. Joe stayed in the hospital until about six p.m. and then left to do his farm chores. Having babies is woman's work!

Sue's night was long and painful and it was not until the next morning that a son was born. Joe came to visit and brought a dozen red roses which were appreciated. The nurse gave him a gown which he figured out how to tie. Sue asked if he wanted to hold his son. He came to the bed and stretched his two arms straight forward at shoulder height and expected Sue to deposit the babe on his outstretched arms. She had to tell him to bend his elbow and cuddle the babe. Joe had never held a baby before. Holding babies is mostly woman's work.

In the beginning of the third year of their marriage Joe and Sue were expecting another baby in September. Sue had been driving the ton truck in late August with the seat pushed back as far as it would go and her very pregnant belly still hitting the steering wheel. The one-year-old son was in a full child seat belted in. The brothers had almost finished picking up bales east of the barn, the truck stopping and starting continuously all the while in first gear. It was almost a full load seven decks high. At the top of the hill looking down to the shore with a quarter mile or more of hills sloping steeply to the water, Sue found no grab in the brake pedal. She hollered to Joe up on the full load to jump down. She turned the truck a bit sideways and fortunately it stopped. Joe told Sue to get out which she did and ran around to the car seat and took it and their son out. She walked to the barnyard and took her Jeep home. Joe crept the truck to the barn. [Getting the work done was more important than safety.]

Joe had ordered five sheep which had been imported from Scotland and had been in quarantine in Mabou for some time. The day Sue's labour pains started, Joe had to drive at least an hour and forty five minutes to Mabou and load the sheep in the back of the ton truck whose brakes had been replaced. Sue had tossed and turned most of the night. Joe got up earlier than usual, had a coffee, and was in the yard building a box on top of the steel sides at five in the morning to contain the sheep. He came in for breakfast of bacon and eggs which Sue had cooked, and said he had to go. He told Sue to call his mother and that his brother Sam would be home until ten or eleven o'clock when he would leave to deliver eggs in town.

Sue did the dishes and took a shower. She did not wish to wake her mother in law, so she waited until after seven a.m. to phone. When Sue picked up the phone, it was dead. So was the battery in her Jeep parked headed downhill in the drive way. Sue shifted the Jeep into fourth gear and popped the clutch halfway down the drive way. She had to park near the cow barn where the driveway was steep enough to pop the clutch to return home. Sue walked to the farmhouse, told her mother in law she was in labour, and asked her to look on the railing of the deck for a large red blanket. That meant she should send Sam over to take her to the hospital.

Sue popped the clutch and drove home. Her pains were about seven minutes apart. She was unsure what time Joe would arrive with the sheep. She made dinner for him, but did not want to eat, a sure sign the baby would arrive within hours. Finally about one-thirty p.m. Joe arrived and parked the truck with the five sheep near the sheep barn and walked home. He wanted dinner before he went anywhere. About four p.m. Joe took Sue to the hospital. It's a good thing Sue had slow labours as the drive to the hospital was still on gravel roads half of the way and took a good thirty minutes. Sue met the nurse at the hospital who told her all the phones for twenty miles along the road Sue and Joe lived on were out of service; a backhoe nearer the town end had accidentally cut the underground phone cables. A few had been fixed but not all.

Just past midnight, Sue's second son arrived. The doctor asked if Sue wanted to phone anyone. The nurse handed her the phone and she dialed home. No ring. Sue phoned her parents in the States and told them the good news. Then she phoned a neighbour who lived further up the road than Sue and Joe did. The phone rang and a grumpy sleepy neighbour said he would go up in the morning and tell Joe he had another son. The phone company billed Sue and Joe for the three days that they had no service. Sue was angry about the nerve of the company to bill for those three days without service and said so to a woman who finally agreed after hearing Sue's problems with delivering her son. [Sometimes you win.]

Sue met Joe in the hen barn, he proposed in the sheep barn, they married when the haying was finished, and their two sons were lucky to be born. And that was only the beginning three years.

*****

Roberta Fraser has worn many hats during her life as teacher, librarian, office clerk, flower shop employee, gas distributor´s cash collector, and farmer. Three things have become the tripod of her life experiences, a love for her grandparents who allowed her to be herself as a child, a love of gardening and a love of animals. Add innate curiosity and fond memories to the tripod. Now that arthritis has settled in and she can no longer turn over the garden by hand, she dons a new hat, writer of humorous events; enjoy them.

The Care and Feeding of Superhero Pets

by Samantha Grandy

The volume of her music had been up too high, blocking the sound of the destruction behind her, and Amy hadn't heard the man calling. She hadn't even known he'd been there until he tapped her on the shoulder. Yanking out a headphone she looked up at him. The sunburnt man grinned down at her, waving his far too expensive digital camera in her face.

"Yes?" Amy asked, raising a brow.

"That's Azeban, huh? It's Azeban and Pryralis, yeah?" The man's words came out in an accented rush, proving he was indeed a tourist. As if his brightly coloured shirt, floppy hat, and fanny pack hadn't given that away

125

already. Amy nodded and the man clapped his hands in delight. "Can you get a picture of me and them?"

Amy tilted her head. In what world did you interrupt someone wearing headphones to ask for a photo? She spied the tour bus behind the man. A large collection of tourists stood beside it while the guide waved energetically towards the fight happening above them. This fight between the superhero and villain had drawn a large crowd, probably since it was located right in the middle of a popular mall plaza. Amy herself had stopped watching about an hour ago when Azeban had grabbed Pyralis mid-air and tossed him into one of the best coffee shops in the city, which he had then lit on fire.

"I suppose?"

The man beamed, tossing his camera to Amy, which she only just caught before it hit the ground. This camera probably cost more than her rent and here was this guy just throwing it. The man looked over at the pair of figures zipping through the sky and then began to try to position himself accordingly, taking off his hat and fixing his hair.

"My kids love them," he told her as she put the notebooks she had been studying on the bench. "My daughter and my son didn't talk for a week after one of their fights, because my daughter has a crush on Pyralis and my son likes Azeban. They got over it though when my daughter bought an Azeban Halloween costume. I never thought I'd get to see them while I was here!"

Indeed, Azeban and Pyralis were popular as the resident superhero and villain. They'd shown up two years ago and since then their popularity had grown, so much that people often visited their city in hopes of getting a glimpse of the heroes. First Pyralis had shown up in his red and black suit, fire powers and all. He'd been loved by almost everyone when he had first appeared, defending the environment, destroying machines or construction sites that were set to go into the woods or the ocean. Soon, though, the power went to his head. Pyralis had started targeting the people in charge of the companies he'd previously been attacking. His behaviour became erratic, with little care for onlookers' safety, and he quickly lost the crowd's support. Of course, there were still people out there who loved him regardless. Only a few months after that, Azeban had appeared, a superhero clad completely in black. Her powers seemed to lie more in illusions and tricks, and she had quickly taken up the superhero mantle that Pyralis had lost. She became the hero to his villain, looking out for the people and trying to protect them from Pyralis.

"Cool," Amy replied. She didn't mean to be rude to the man, but he didn't get to be excited about their superheroes and then get to leave to go to another place that had a coffee shop not destroyed by said superheroes. "You ready?"

"Oh, one minute!" The man unzipped the neon fanny pack around his waist and reached into it, gingerly pulling out a small brass vase. He held it up next to his face. "Okay, ready!"

Amy adjusted the camera, making sure she got the man in the frame along with the two figures in the background. She snapped a few photos and then held the camera out for him to take it back. The man took it with one hand and began to flip through the photos, still holding the vase close to his face.

"Oh, that looks like Facebook profile material, doesn't it, Beth?" The man chuckled.

"I beg your pardon?"

"Oh, I was just talking to my wife, Beth." The man tipped his head toward the vase in his hand. "Had to take her on the trip with me—well, not all of her of course, the kids have the rest of her."

Oh my god.

His wife.

His wife was in the vase—no, the *urn*, Amy supposed.

She watched in muted horror as the man smiled, thanked her for the photo and then crammed his wife back into his fanny-pack. This man had just put his wife in the most god-awful accessory to come out of the 80's/90's and then had the gall to walk away like nothing had happened.

A loud collective gasp from the crowd drew her attention away from the man, and she turned just in time to see Azeban throw Pyralis to the ground with an ear-shattering bang. A ring of fire erupted around Pyralis and Amy sighed, throwing her backpack over her shoulders and turning to walk back to the car. The tourists were all still hooked, but most of the locals in the crowd started to disperse. They knew as well as she did that the fight was pretty much over. If things went as they typically did, by the time the fire died down Pyralis would be gone, the police would step in, and Azeban would either get caught up making statements or be free to go, depending on the amount of damage the two had caused.

The walk to the car wasn't long; Lola had only parked a few blocks over from where Amy had been studying. In a few minutes Amy was unlocking the doors to the beat-up green Toyota and folding herself into the passenger seat. The car, however, wasn't vacant; as soon as she closed the door she was met by a chirping sound.

"Jesus Christ," she hissed and glanced over to see the raccoon peering up at her from the driver's seat. "Did you just leave Lola and come to the car?"

Of course the raccoon didn't answer her. He continued to stare up at her with his large brown eyes and paw at her pant leg, before crawling onto her lap and pulling greedily at her bag, which she'd thrown down by her feet. Amy leaned down, opening the bag for the creature, who expertly pulled out a plastic bag of trail mix and dried berries and wandered back over to the driver's seat with it.

Amy took out her phone, sending a quick text to her friend to let her know that she currently had custody of their third roommate, the raccoon. She got a text back almost instantly telling her that Lola had sent him back to her purposely, so she was well aware of his location.

Minutes later, Lola threw her door open, picked up the raccoon and his bag, and deposited him on Amy's lap before crawling into the car herself. Her dark hair was tied in a poor excuse for a ponytail, with strands falling out around her face, making it look like she'd run all the way to the car.

"You've got soot on your face," Amy said helpfully as she handed Lola the keys.

Lola let out a low curse, flipping the rear-view mirror to get a better look at herself and scrubbing furiously at her right cheek with her sleeve. "Stupid Pyralis."

"Didn't have fun today, Azeban?" Amy asked. The raccoon looked up at her and chattered around a mouthful of dried strawberries. "No, not you, her."

Having your best friend's superhero identity and raccoon spirit share the same name sometimes got confusing.

"Tons of fun. I think he fractured three of my ribs," Lola groaned as she started the car. "If I cough up blood tonight though I'm not going to the hospital."

"Karma for killing the best coffee shop on this side of the city," Amy muttered, petting the raccoon in her lap.

"Okay, it was either the coffee shop or the youth centre."

"It's nice out, the kids can go outside."

"You're a monster."

"My kindness is fueled by my caffeine intake. This is your fault. You created this, so congratulations, Doctor Frankenstein."

"You'll be the next villain I have to fend off."

"How was Pyralis today, anyway?"

Lola's lips pressed together and her brow furrowed. She took a moment before speaking. "I'm tired of him escaping like that. Pyralis is getting way more sporadic; I can't predict his movements and his plans like I used to." She let out a long sigh. "I don't know. I just wish I could understand what was happening."

"Sounds like you and your arch-enemy need some couples counselling," Amy snickered. Her laughter died under Lola's withering glare. "Okay, fine, no jokes. In reality, it's probably getting more difficult because your fan base is growing and so is his. It's like a rally every time the two of you fight. The police are left doing traffic control instead of helping."

"The fans are getting a little too intense. We might have to send out a memo to get them to calm down." Lola shrugged. "There were some with posters out today."

"Oh, you don't even want to know about

the fan of yours that I encountered today."

Lola winced. "A cosplayer?"

"Worse. A dead body."

"Wait, what?"

"Exactly."

As they drove, Amy gave Lola the quick version of the notes she had studied, so her friend would be caught up on classwork. Lola, in return, gave Amy more details of the recent fight. Azeban, the raccoon, stayed on Amy's lap gleefully chewing on the berries and nuts.

"Does she not feed you, Azeban?" Amy cooed as she stroked the creature's back, ignoring how his claws dug into her thigh and all the fur he was shedding on her shirt.

"Oh, he eats all right," Lola hissed. "He's a pudding fiend."

"He is a mystical creature, leave him be."

Azeban squeaked, large brown eyes turning to look at Amy as he held the bag in one paw. He'd somehow got the bag twisted in his excitement and now his paw couldn't go down all the way to get the berries at the bottom. Amy unwound the bag and Azeban made a satisfied noise before resuming his feast. In all honesty, you would never guess he was a mystical beast or a spirit from stories parents told their children at night. He seemed like a docile raccoon when his power wasn't active, albeit a little mischievous and a pain when he was in the mood.

Lola had called Amy frantically when she first found the creature, not knowing what to do with him considering she hadn't even been able to keep her pet goldfish alive for a day. Azeban had proven to be fairly self-sufficient; however, he did love when they indulged him and had taken a keen liking to being spoiled by Amy. He had entered their lives several months before Lola had taken up her superhero title. She had been visiting her grandmother in Quebec, helping pack up some of her grandfather's things. Lola had banged into one of the boxes when she was alone and shattered a clay figurine, and all of a sudden this raccoon was staring up at her. Of course, Azeban being a low-level trickster spirit had decided to disappear every time someone else was around and reappear whenever Lola was alone. No matter where she was, somehow Azeban would find his way there as well.

Lola came home with Azeban and a few of her grandfather's journals. She and Amy quickly went to work, trying to figure out exactly how they had gotten hold of a magical raccoon. They learned he was a trickster spirit from the myths and legends of the Abenaki people; Lola's heritage through her grandparents and mother. Lola's grandfather claimed he bought the figurine because the seller said it contained a piece of the spirit's soul as punishment for his misdoings. He'd suspected it was a way to jack up the price, but he'd bought it anyway.

A little more research revealed that Azeban wasn't a malevolent or evil spirit, just a trickster who wanted to have fun and pull harmless pranks. In the mythology, he was responsible for the raccoon's black mask because of the tricks he'd played on two blind men. He had once gotten into a shouting match with a waterfall, which they had learned only after Azeban almost mauled them when they tried to put him in the tub with the tap still running. After that particular instance they had started reading up on every myth they could find about the spirit and compiling all the knowledge into a binder so they wouldn't be blindsided again.

Nobody else knew about Azeban's existence. They'd kept the secret, first, to avoid mental hospitals, and later, to keep Lola's superhero identity a secret, like every other superhero in the movies they had mocked.

Going through her phone now, Amy flipped through notifications she'd ignored earlier, noticing a few likes on a photo she had taken last night of Azeban lying across her bed. She'd tagged it with his Instagram handle @banditlooncoon, Bandit being the fake name they had assigned him to avoid awkward questions about myths and superheroes. One particular "like" caught Amy's eye, though.

"My coffee shop liked the photo I posted," Amy muttered. "Commented on it too, saying they couldn't wait for my next visit and hoped I'd bring Bandit."

Lola winced, not looking over. "I'm sorry, okay?"

"I was a stamp away from getting a free drink."

"Look, I'll buy you all the coffee you want!"

"Okay, one: with what money? Two: from where? You made the best coffee shop explode into a million pieces!"

Lola let her head fall back against the seat and rolled her eyes. "I'm sorry! From the deepest bottom of my heart I apologize for murdering your one true love: caffeine."

"I'll remember this," Amy muttered as she picked up Azeban. He made a small noise of protest before turning into putty in her arms as she nuzzled her face against his fur. "Just you wait, vengeance will be mine."

"What are you going to do, exactly?" Lola asked, and when she was met with silence she sighed. "Seriously though, I killed your coffee shop, you're going to ruin my life sometime in the future, but can we put all that aside because I need to get gas ASAP. You'll go splits on it with me, right?"

"I suppose," Amy answered as if it weren't a rhetorical question.

Muttering as she hunted for a gas station, Lola drove and Amy continued to pet Azeban, occasionally taking out a handful of berries for the raccoon to munch. His energy dipped after a fight and he was always a little off after Lola drew from his powers. They didn't understand how the transition worked; nothing in their research explained it. Azeban was a trickster spirit, so all his magic used illusion. He would tuck himself away somewhere when Lola fought, turning invisible as Lola drew on his power. Mostly everything she could do—aside from the strength, ability to fly, and invulnerability—was pretty much just a trick of the eyes, Azeban's specialty. Lola and Azeban had a deep connection Amy could never understand.

Eventually Lola found a gas station and pulled up to a pump. She glanced at the now-empty bag of berries and the drowsy Azeban as she shut off the car. "I guess we need to get somebody some more snacks."

Whether it was the mention of snacks, or the car pulling up at the pump beside them, Azeban shot up. He chattered as he leaned up to peer out the passenger window. The two girls followed his gaze to see the green smart car parked next to them. The driver, a blond man, glanced over and waved. Lola instantly paled and turned her head to Amy.

"Please tell me that isn't Hayden. Can you please tell me I'm seeing things and that isn't him?"

"I could," Amy answered, peering back at the man who was getting out of his car. "But that would be a lie."

"For god's sake," Lola hissed and ran a hand through her hair.

Amy rolled her eyes. "Go get Azeban some snacks and pay for the gas. I'll pump it." She grabbed the raccoon and plopped him in the back seat so she could get out of the car.

"Maybe I can be your wing woman."

"Amy, don't you dare or you'll be walking everywhere for the foreseeable future. You can't even set up a Kinder Surprise toy, let alone a relationship," Lola warned, her face nearing scarlet now as she grabbed her wallet.

Amy gave a shrug as Lola glared at her once more before hopping out of the car and quickly running to the entrance of the gas station. She made no eye contact with anyone, let alone Hayden. Amy waited until her friend was inside and then got out of the car and began to pump the gas.

"Hey, Amy." Hayden nodded at her. "Was that Lola who just ran off?"

"Yeah, had to grab something really quick."

Hayden just smiled at her, his smile so wide that it made his green eyes squint. Lola had been infatuated with him for almost a year after meeting him at one of Amy's Science Society meetings. Amy and Hayden were in the same program, so in turn they had a lot of the same classes. He was a nice guy and Amy considered him a school friend. She assumed he considered her a little strange because he had caught her taking photos of him a few times (Snapchats for Lola in return for not having to pay for gas those weeks).

"Didn't peg you for a smart car owner," Amy said, nodding her head to his tiny green car.

Hayden only chuckled. "It's easy on gas and gets me where I need to go. I've been dying to buy one of those rechargeable cars, but you know; poor college kid."

"Story of my life."

Hayden's brows furrowed and his smile faltered as he looked over Amy's shoulder. "Am I crazy, or is there a raccoon in your car?"

Amy followed his gaze to see Azeban peering out the back window at the two of them. She couldn't hear him, but could see his mouth moving and paws scraping against the window. He'd duck down, do a spin and then pop back up.

"No, that's Bandit," Amy answered, looking back to Hayden. "Lola's pet."

"Pet raccoon?"

"Long story short, we found him as a baby, his mom had been hit by a car and he ended up basically imprinting on Lola," Amy explained, using the cover story they had created. In all honesty it wouldn't even be the weirdest pet this city had seen. A woman in their apartment building owned a pet goat and dressed it up differently every day, and Amy had also encountered a therapy Komodo dragon one summer while working at an ice cream shop.

As Hayden continued to stare, Amy really hoped he wouldn't mention that it was technically illegal to keep a raccoon as a pet in the province of Ontario. It wasn't an extremely well-known fact and when it did come up, well, Azeban had used his magic to get around those situations.

Whether Hayden knew this information or was even interested in it became completely irrelevant as he looked over Amy's shoulder again, giving a lopsided smirk. He lifted his free hand and waved.

"Hey Lola," he called in a low voice. Amy turned her head to see her friend walking out of the gas station with bags in her arms.

"Hi," Lola muttered, fumbling with her groceries and looking like a deer in the headlights. "Fancy meeting you here, what brings you to the gas station?"

Oh god, she was going to try to flirt. Amy tried not to wince.

"Getting gas?" Hayden answered and Amy was pretty sure she wasn't imagining how his cheeks were turning red.

"Oh yeah, me too! Got to love having gas! I mean getting gas...for a car, not for me as a person." Lola tripped over her words, talking too fast. Amy was just about to forgive her for destroying the coffee shop, because honestly no revenge would be worse than the torture Lola was currently putting herself through.

Amy reached over and put the nozzle back in its place. Azeban continued to run circles in the car, stopping to paw desperately at the window. "What's wrong with him?" Amy asked.

Lola looked over. "Probably knows I have his treats."

Amy laughed and took the snacks from Lola, opening the door and hopping into the backseat with Azeban. The raccoon climbed onto her lap, pawing at the bag as Amy tried to open it. She left the car door open so she could clearly see and hear Hayden and Lola. She watched as Hayden approached Lola and as Lola seemed to just shut down mentally the closer he got.

"Lola's got a crush," Amy whisper-sang to Azeban as he picked some cashews out of her hand. He didn't pause in his eating but he looked up at his superhero partner and made a small chittering noise.

They stayed like that for several minutes, Amy sitting in the car feeding Azeban as Hayden and Lola stood outside talking. Amy listened just in case Lola got too flustered, or said something extremely stupid and needed Amy's intervention. Amy heard a touch of panic in Lola's voice as she suddenly pitched the idea of Hayden officially meeting Azeban. As they approached, Azeban's attention shifted solely to them instead of the food.

"So he's harmless, right?" Hayden asked, as he slowly reached out to pet the raccoon. Azeban let out a feral screech, digging his claws into Amy's legs before using her as a launch pad and jumping out of the car.

"Bandit, what the hell?" Lola yelled as she scurried after the raccoon. Amy jumped out of the car to help.

Azeban had backed up to an iron fence leading to an alleyway. He spared the three of them a glance before turning and slipping under the fence. He didn't look back as he sprinted out of view, ducking around a turn.

"Holy shit! Lola, what do we do?"

"I'm so sorry, Lola," Hayden blurted. "I didn't mean to scare him. I'm sorry."

"It's nobody's fault," Amy told Hayden with a forced smile. "I shouldn't have had the door open like that. He's never acted that way though, so how were we to know?"

"Amy's right," Lola said calmly, but Amy could see the panic in her eyes. "I need to run home to grab some...stuff to lure him back. Amy, can you start looking for him? I'll text when I'm on my way back."

Amy knew Lola must be going for the binder. The raccoon had gone off as if he were terrified, so there could be a clue about why in their research. He might be an ancient spirit, but in appearance he was still a raccoon running the streets of the city, and that was dangerous. They mustn't scare him off again if they did find him.

Hayden had kept running his hands through his hair and apologizing. "I'll help!" he chimed in nervously. "It's the least I can do. It's my fault he ran off."

"Okay, come with me," Amy said as she walked back to the car for her things, stepping over the scattered and broken remains of the cashews. "I'm going to run to the store and get him some snacks."

Lola waited while Amy grabbed her stuff. She shot Hayden a weak smile and whispered to Amy, "I might try to use my powers if we can't find him. You'll have to distract Hayden."

Amy nodded. "I can do that. We need to get Azeban before something else does."

They shared one last worried look before Lola climbed in and drove off.

After the quick trip to the grocery store down the road Amy had a bag of fresh berries, pudding cups, and a package of mini marshmallows. Hayden had veered off for a few minutes and came back with his own armload of first aid supplies. Amy had only given him a questioning look but didn't bother to ask; Hayden had a reputation in the Science Society as a mother hen. He fretted over every safety procedure and was constantly making sure that everyone followed the rules with extra precautions at all times.

On the way back, Amy noticed how every time Lola's name came up in conversation, Hayden would blush and give a shy smile before catching himself. Finally he asked, "So what do we do if we see Bandit?"

"Show him a pudding cup or some marshmallows," Amy answered as the lights of the gas station came into view.

"Really?"

"He loves pudding; Lola was getting annoyed about it earlier, actually."

"You've known each other for a long time, haven't you? You and Lola, I mean."

"We've been friends since junior high." They'd met when they'd been forced to be partners in English class. "It was just dumb luck that we got into the same university, we didn't plan it. But it works in our favour for not having to worry about annoying roommates."

"You guys are lucky to have been friends for so long." Hayden smiled down at her. "I don't even talk to half the people I knew in high school, let alone junior high."

"You should really hang out with us sometime," she said and watched Hayden stumble on the even pavement of the entrance to the gas station. His crush on Lola was pretty cute. "I'm sure Lola would love it."

"I don't know, I wouldn't want to impose on you guys," Hayden muttered.

"You wouldn't be. Lola's mentioned inviting you out with us a few times." Not actually a lie, but Lola's statements had been more hypothetical musings.

"Really?"

"Yeah," Amy answered and then looked around. "Okay, so this is where we lost him."

Hayden walked over to the fence where Azeban had disappeared. "He went under here."

"Okay, but how do we get over there?"

"Jump." Hayden looked down at her. He quirked his eyebrows at the annoyed expression Amy gave him. "What? You don't think you can jump over it?"

"That was a short joke, and I can't say I'm fond of those," she answered dryly. Hayden only chuckled in response; she was getting tired of hanging around giants who thought

5'2" was small. Amy turned her attention back to the fence. "Honestly, I couldn't get over this if I tried. We'll have to find another way to get back there."

Hayden walked over to the fence and gave it a good shake. It barely moved. Hayden smiled and knelt next to the fence, cupping his hands in front of him. "All right."

"All right? All right what?"

"I'm going to boost you over."

Amy's eyes widened as she looked at Hayden's hands. "You've got to be kidding me," she whispered. She *really* looked at Hayden again and took in his slim frame, the fact that he had slender hands—not sturdy, hefting-a-grown-woman-over-a-fence kind of hands. His face, however, was determined. "No, Hayden. I'll break you. "I'm not trying to hurt your masculinity. I just seriously don't want to hurt *you* physically."

"I'm stronger than I look. Amy, you've met me. Do you really think I'd be doing this if I thought there was a risk of injury to either of us? Seriously come on, just step on my hands so we can start looking for that raccoon."

Well, his dedication to finding Lola's pet seemed genuine at least.

Hesitantly, she placed her bags next to the fence so Hayden could pass them to her in the unlikely event this went well. Carefully she put her right foot in Hayden's hands.

"I'm not going to break, Amy, come on."

She relented and grabbed the top of the

fence. Hayden boosted. To her astonishment with just a twist of her body she was over the fence and safely on her feet, peering in shock through the bars at Hayden.

"Told you." Hayden said as he passed her bags through the bars. He backed up, ran to the fence, and swung himself over, landing perfectly on his feet.

Well, damn. "Way to show off."

"You're impressed, don't lie. All right, let's look for Bandit. How do you want to do this?"

Amy pulled out one of the bags of mini marshmallows and two pudding cups, handing them to him. She took out a bag of trail mix and a separate bag of assorted berries and opened them both. "You have a flashlight on your phone, right? It'll be easier to check under things, plus it'll be getting dark soon."

"It's 2018, of course I have a flashlight on my phone," Hayden replied, holding the food in one hand and fishing his phone out of his pocket with the other. He swiped the flashlight on.

They walked down the alley, checking under dumpsters, nudging boxes, abandoned furniture or anything a raccoon could hide in or under. A few false alarms turned out to be stray cats. The alley jutted out at odd angles, with old boxes and furniture all over the place. If she was mapping out their location correctly, then this path led them behind a few abandoned restaurants and businesses, and it seemed as though most of those places had just thrown everything out into the alleyway, rather than bothering to actually get rid of it when they closed down. Even the fire escapes were littered with boxes and precariously piled furniture, as if they couldn't find enough space on the ground to put it all.

"Jesus, the mess," Hayden muttered.

Amy nodded. Of course Azeban would choose this way. He was a trickster and this place offered more hiding places, more chances for illusions, more opportunity for general mischievousness. He would pick the more complicated path because to him, unlike every other creature, this path would bring him comfort with all its chaos. But she couldn't tell Hayden any of that.

Amy scattered a few berries, and Hayden did the same with the marshmallows. They were only about halfway down this path when a high and peppy piano riff rang out. They both jumped. Hayden swore. Amy looked over to see him picking up the bag of marshmallows and collecting the ones that had escaped. The riff continued. Amy's home screen lit up with a less-than-flattering photo of her best friend.

"It's just Lola," she told Hayden. He stood, one hand clutching the bag of marshmallows and the other pressed over his heart. Amy looked down at the text. "She says from what she Googled, Azeban's probably hiding out in a tiny spot somewhere, or trying to find food."

"Why did you even have Bandit out with you?

"We were studying in the park," Amy answered, the half-lie coming easily since she had been studying before this whole mess occurred. "Lola took Bandit with us because he loves being outside. Anyway, I'm sure you've seen the news that Azeban and Pyralis got into another fight and we were close by, so we decided to go check it out."

"You were at the fight?" Hayden's voice was low. "Didn't the police release a statement last month that people needed to stop going to those because of the danger?"

"Yeah, but it's interesting to watch." She shrugged, pretending she hadn't had this same conversation with Lola only hours before. "What do you think of Azeban, anyway?"

Hayden snorted. "She's a little overrated, don't you think?"

"A superhero is overrated?"

"No, I mean she says she's for the people and everything, but she has no problem destroying things or putting people in danger in order to stop Pyralis. They call her a hero but really, she's as much of an inconvenience as he is." Hayden's back was suddenly straight, his eyes avoiding Amy as he began to move forward again, shining his light and kicking boxes out of his way. "You must see that?"

The coffee shop. Her favourite coffee shop had been murdered in cold blood today, but as much as Amy wanted to agree that the destruction was unnecessary, she couldn't.

"It's either that or let Pyralis torch the whole place. Azeban is only doing what's necessary to save people. She's never once harmed anybody. Sure, things get destroyed sometimes, but in the end it's to keep everyone safe."

"Safe from what, exactly?" Hayden asked with a cock of his head. "I mean there have been instances where Pyralis has hurt people, but it's only because they've been in the wrong places at the wrong time, or because they were in the wrong."

"You're not seriously defending him?" Sweet innocent Hayden, Hayden who acted like an overbearing mother hen in labs trying to make sure everyone was okay and safe at all times. That same Hayden was defending Pyralis? And he was totally not a fan of her best friend's alter-ego.

"I am," he answered with a shrug. "He deserves more recognition then he gets. What can I say? I'm a fan."

"A fan of a psychopa—" Amy began, but was interrupted by a scuffling noise. It came from the box Hayden had just kicked.

The argument was forgotten and Hayden gently toed the box. More scuffling. Before Amy could move Hayden lifted the box carefully to reveal a small creature huddled underneath. Hayden shined his light down on Azeban, who made a small noise of protest and tried to scramble away.

"That's him!"

Hayden dove for the raccoon and Azeban shrieked and darted off, not far but out of reach. Amy studied Azeban and he seemed no worse for the wear, a little dirty and in need of a bath, but unharmed. The raccoon's brown eyes met Amy's and she noticed his heaving chest as he gulped breath after breath. Hayden made another move toward him and Azeban growled, the fur on his back standing straight up as he backed away from the man.

"Hayden stop, you're scaring him!" Amy rummaged through the plastic bags, desperate to find something that would draw Azeban's attention to her instead of Hayden.

"I'm scaring him?" Hayden snapped back, but he stopped walking towards the still-snarling raccoon. "Does this thing have all his shots?"

"Absolutely." Amy answered automatically. Of course it was a lie. How in god's name were they supposed to take an all-powerful spirit to the vet in order to get a needle for some disease he probably couldn't even get? "Just stay where you are, he won't hurt you."

Hayden did as he was told and Azeban stayed where he was, still making feral warning sounds. Amy had never seen him react this way, but Azeban didn't have a lot of encounters with men, or strangers in general. He was probably just spooked.

Amy dug a pudding cup out of her bag and began to peel back the lid, slowly approaching the raccoon. Azeban's eyes darted from

Hayden to Amy, finally settling on Amy. He made a small sound of relief. His eyes narrowed in on the pudding cup, but he wouldn't dare move towards her, eyes snapping back to Hayden every time he twitched.

"Do you want me to try to grab him?" Hayden whispered.

"Definitely not." She crouched so Azeban could see and smell the pudding. "Hey buddy, look what I've got for you."

Azeban chittered in response, looking at Hayden warily before his eyes finally shifted back to Amy. He took a hesitant step past Hayden and towards her, as if all he wanted was to get to Amy and the pudding, but no part of him wanted to walk by Hayden. Azeban took another painfully slow step, looking again at Hayden and letting out a displeased chatter before he took another step.

Amy placed a hand on the ground to steady herself as she offered the cup and smiled. "That's a good raccoon, c'mon, just come to Amy so we can go home." Her eyes quickly darted to Hayden to make sure he was staying put. His eyes were almost as wide as the raccoon's.

Four feet, that's all the distance there was between Amy and Azeban, four feet and this whole mess would be over. Or it would have been, if one of the stray cats hadn't chosen that moment to squeeze out a broken window and let out a long low hiss at Azeban. The calico crouched, swaying its tail from side to side.

"Shit," Hayden whispered.

Amy tried to make a move for the cat without scaring Azeban, but it was too late. The cat lunged for the raccoon and Azeban had the good sense not to reveal his powers in front of Hayden. Instead he darted off in the opposite direction, running past Hayden and far out of Amy's reach. The cat only ran a few feet after him. Then she seemed satisfied to have the raccoon out of sight, and took a delicate strut around the area, reclaiming her territory.

"Are you kidding me?" Amy hissed, throwing the pudding cup to the ground and watching the stray run to eagerly lick up the remains. She glared at the cat. "I hope you're happy with yourself."

"We almost had him." Hayden sighed, glancing around the alleyway. He gestured in the direction Azeban had gone. "What now?"

"We follow him," Amy said, holding back her tears of frustration. They had just been so close.

"All right, how about I keep an eye on the fire escapes and the edges of the roofs. Maybe we'll see him running around there," Hayden said with a small reassuring smile. "I mean, since you can't see that high."

"Haha, another short joke, very funny. You know, I used to think you were a nice guy," Amy muttered, but did crack the tiniest smile. "I still can't believe you're a Pyralis fanboy though, you still seem too nice for that."

"I didn't realize you had to be evil to like Pyralis?"

"I know you said that he never hurt anyone or ruined anything intentionally, but still he's destroyed things and has hurt the general public. And a few times he's beat the living hell out of Azeban." She knew there had been times when Pyralis would have killed Azeban without a second thought if he had the chance. She'd been the one to patch Lola up, after all. Or even force her to go to the hospital after Pyralis had gotten the better of her.

"Yes, but that works both ways, if you want to use that argument." Hayden's voice was calm but detached. "Azeban has always seemed to return the favour without hesitation. From my viewpoint, Pyralis is just a guy trying to do what he thinks is right. Everybody used to support him before the media turned on him, and if you ignore them then he's still a good guy trying to help the environment."

"But he's going about it the wrong way."

"Maybe that's the only way he knows how to do it?"

"I think this is going to be one of those moments where we have to agree to disagree," Amy muttered, suddenly wanting to drop the subject. It was getting too intense.

"Fair enough."

Amy's phone pinged. She quickly read the message and typed back her response. "That was Lola. She just got back to the gas station, so I told her where we were and she's going to come around the other way to look for Bandit and meet us." Amy pocketed her phone. She'd left out the parts where Lola was going to try to use her connection with Azeban to locate him, and also climb around a bit on the roofs to get a better look. Amy hoped Azeban would pick up on Lola's presence and go to her; she also hoped Hayden wouldn't look *too* closely at the roofs.

Hayden cleared his throat awkwardly. "Hey, this is going to be a really weird question, especially considering the conversation we just had—and we can forget it ever happened—but is Lola seeing anyone?"

"She has eyes, Hayden, she sees lots of people." Amy smirked. That was for the short jokes.

"You know what I mean," he muttered, turning his attention from her to stare up at an old couch balanced on the fire escape above them.

"If you're asking if she's single then yes, she is." Amy laughed, noticing how Hayden dipped his head down and smiled. "It's okay if you like her, that's fine. I have it on good authority that she thinks you're a pretty good guy too."

"Really? What has she said about me?" he asked, gently kicking the bottom of a large stack of boxes.

"Okay, no. I'm her best friend, so we're not having this conversation where I betray her trust," Amy said, raising her hand to stop his rambling. "I'm just saying if you want to take your shot, it's not hopeless."

Hayden looked up and fully smiled at her this time, then turned back to give the box another gentle kick. A cat ran out from behind the box and climbed the stack, leaping from that to the fire escape. It caught the edge of the old couch above Amy's head, claws scrabbling on the worn fabric, and swung its body onto the couch's overhanging end. As if in slow motion, the couch began to tip. The cat catapulted off it onto the next fire escape, dislodging yet another stack of boxes which tumbled onto the now-falling furniture.

She knew she should run, jump, get out of the way; but despite the feeling of slow motion, Amy couldn't seem to move. As the couch toppled toward her, she squeezed her eyes shut, waiting for impact.

After several seconds, though, there was nothing but a slight tingle on her face and arms and the smell of smoke. Hesitantly she cracked open an eye to see white and black ash falling from the sky. No couch in sight. Only Hayden, with his eyes wide and his hand outstretched.

It took her longer than she would like to admit to piece it all together. Her brain felt slow and fuzzy with all of this new information at once. She stared at Hayden. He stared back at her, his face pale and lips pulled together in a thin line. Her gaze traveled to his outstretched hand and the flames; tiny flames licking at the tips of his fingers. She met his eyes as the pieces clicked.

"You can't tell anyone," Hayden whispered.

"You're Pyralis," Amy answered, the words flying out of her mouth as the light bulb flicked on in her head.

"Amy, seriously, you can't tell anyone," Hayden hissed. He took a step closer, and she saw that even though he spoke calmly his eyes were frantic and searching her face. "Nobody knows who I am and nobody can know."

"You're a supervillain," she muttered more to herself. "I've seen you cry over videos of puppies getting rescued, but you're a supervillain."

Hayden made a noise in the back of his throat that sounded like an animal in pain. "I'm not a villain, we already talked about this! I'm still me! I've tried to explain it before. As Pyralis I only go after people who are hurting us, people who are trying to kill everything!"

"You've caused millions of dollars in damage, you've hurt people and you've attacked the city!" Amy countered. She tried to piece together everything she knew about Pyralis and everything she knew about Hayden, but it didn't want to fit.

"You're getting the wrong side of the story; I'm doing what's right!"

"Hayden," Amy said softly, taking a step towards him.

"I don't want to hurt you." Hayden took a

step back and his hand ignited in a brilliant orange flame. It lit up the area around them. "I don't—you're my friend, but you can't tell anyone! Please, nobody can know who I am! Please, Amy!"

Amy had dealt with enough secrets for Lola that she knew how to mask her face. Hayden was a sweet guy; he was smart and funny, always helping everyone in class and always volunteering when he could. He was a genuinely good person. She didn't want to hurt him, didn't want to do anything that would get him in trouble. However, this was also Pyralis, the bane of her best friends' existence.

"Please, Amy." Hayden's voice sounded desperate.

"All right," she whispered, lifting her head to meet his eyes. "Your secret is safe with me. I'm not doing this for Pyralis, though. You're my friend, Hayden, and I'm doing this for you."

His secret was safe with her—at least until she figured out what to do with all this new information. Maybe she could use her friendship with Hayden to help Pyralis turn over a new leaf and change his ways, or at least the way he went about achieving his goals. Maybe this whole mess could end up working out in her favour if she played it right. She just needed some time to think.

"Thank you." Hayden sighed as his shoulders relaxed, the flames dying off his hand as he let it fall back to his side. "You have no idea how nervous I've been about someone finding out and what they would do."

"How did you become Pyralis?" Amy asked, swallowing her anxiety. She knew Hayden could probably still see the shock that she couldn't completely mask.

Hayden rubbed the back of his neck, clearly still wary. "It's a long, complicated story actually; most of the time it requires me to write it out on chart paper just to keep it straight."

"Hey!" A voice called from further down the alley. They turned to see Lola running towards them, something swaying in her arms. Hayden perked up, and then turned to look at Amy, as if to remind her about their new shared secret. Like she could forget. As Lola approached it was easier to see that the thing in her arms was Azeban. "Look who I found?"

"Where was he?" Amy gasped, running to pet the raccoon in her friend's arms. He chittered at her. "You scared me half to death, you little beast."

"He was sizing up a cat for her can of food near the opening to the street," Lola laughed. "He just ran straight to me when he saw me coming."

Amy smiled back, stroking Azeban's soft head. Well, at least that was one crisis averted. She opened her arms and Lola passed Azeban over, his familiar weight comforting. Amy had worried she might never hug the raccoon again. Lola looked off past Amy and instantly tucked her hair behind her ears.

"Hi," Lola said in a quiet voice.

"Hey." Hayden's tone was almost identical. "I'm glad you found Bandit."

"Yeah, bit of scare there, but thank you for helping." Lola answered with a confidence Amy didn't realize she could possess around Hayden. Maybe this scare had put things into perspective for her.

"Not a problem."

Amy looked up to see Hayden smiling. He shuffled his feet and his hand came up to rub the back of his neck, all traces of his earlier frantic attitude completely gone. "Hey, I was wondering if you wanted to exchange phone numbers so we could hang out sometime, maybe grab a coffee?"

Lola nodded her head vigorously before she answered. "Sure," she replied and tossed her phone to Hayden so he could type in his number. "That sounds great. I love coffee and going out for coffee, not that I do it a lot. I mean, I'm not a hermit or anything. Just that—yes, I would like to go out for coffee with you."

There was the Lola Amy knew, back in full force. Hayden gave her a small smirk as he handed Lola her phone, his own cheeks darkening. Amy noticed how the tips of his fingers seemed to glow for a half a second before he shoved his hands into his pockets. Azeban chirped and slipped out of Amy's grasp. He walked over to Lola, pawing at her leg until she picked him up. Over her shoulder he shot Amy a deliberate look that she couldn't quite decipher. The raccoon's dark eyes almost seemed to be...laughing at her?

"You free Thursday?" Hayden asked. Lola nodded. "It's a date, then."

"This may sound mean," Hayden continued as he reached a tentative hand out to stroke the raccoon's head. Azeban didn't even flinch now. "But I'm kind of happy he ran off. Gave me a chance to talk to you finally."

"Sometimes things just work out in a weird way, I guess." Lola smiled up at Hayden.

Together they turned to walk out of the alleyway. Amy followed, but if they included her in the conversation, she didn't notice. *What just happened?* Azeban hadn't started to act up in the car until Hayden showed up. He'd run away when Amy and Hayden had found him together, but not when Lola had brought him over to Hayden. It was clear from his reaction earlier that Azeban had figured out who Hayden really was before Amy had. But why didn't he seem to care now?

Oh, no.

Amy stopped walking and stared at the couple ahead of her. There was no way that Azeban could have planned this. Sure, he was a trickster spirit and seemed to like making their lives more complicated then necessary. But to go through all that trouble to set up a superhero and her rival supervillain? That seemed extreme. Azeban thrived on chaos, but this was more than that—this was insanity.

No. No way the raccoon had intentionally done this.

Azeban peered over Lola's shoulder at Amy, his face smug and his eyes dancing with amusement.

Amy shook her head. Yeah. He'd known exactly what he was doing. She sighed and ran to catch up. *Crisis averted? Hah! This crisis was only beginning.* She'd have to keep an even closer eye on Azeban from now on.

She didn't really mind. She had no desire to be a superhero herself. But friends with superheroes? That just made life interesting.

*****

Samantha Grandy is from North Sydney, Nova Scotia and was born and raised in Cape Breton and therefore has a major problem with using proper spelling and grammar in regular speech and writing. Relatively new to the Story Forge, she has been writing for fun for over ten years, with countless documents saved to her computer and sent out as e-mails to friends, but this is the first time sharing her work.

Samantha is a school teacher along with being a master at procrastination. When not working, or staring at a blank word document, she is often in a world of her own imagination, reading, taking photos, badly dancing and lip syncing to the radio, spending time with her pets, friends, family, or trying to convince somebody to go for a walk in the woods.

Come-From-Aways

by Sherry D. Ramsey

The day John Allan MacAskill Laidlaw blew
back into town, I was one of the first people to
know about it. That's because I was in Shirl's
chair at *The Hair Net*, getting my monthly cut
and style, when Mrs. Martha Dunvegan puffed
in to share the news that she'd seen him. Not
surprising. Mrs. Martha D. is "in the loop."
Heck, sometimes I think she is the loop.

"Drivin' a car almost as long as the school
bus," Mrs. Martha D. reported with a sniff and
a shake of her well-permed and blued curls.
"And a license plate that says THE MAC. I told
his mother she shouldn't let him get away with
that silliness about changing his name when
he was sixteen, but would she listen to me? No.
What's wrong with John Allan? I said." She
pronounced it *J'nallan*, with a proper Gaelic

lilt. "It's a good, solid name. But no, Mac he became, and no one could tell him different." She paused for breath.

"She always went easy on him," Shirl said, chop-cutting the back of my hair vigorously. "On account of his father, of course."

"Friggin' CFA's," Mrs. Martha D. snorted.

"Mac's not really a come-from-away," I countered meekly. "I mean, he did grow up here. He's probably visiting his mother," I ventured. "Mother's Day is next week."

"*Pfft!*" Mrs. Martha D. blew her breath out between puckered lips. "He hasn't been home in ten years for Mother's Day or that poor woman's birthday *or* Christmas. If that doesn't make him a CFA, I don't know what does. He's forgotten all about his roots."

She turned a piercing blue eye on me. "I hope he's not here to see *you*."

I lifted my chin, but Shirl pushed my head forward again to keep cutting, so the gesture lost its effect. "Hardly," I muttered into my chest. "I want nothing to do with Mac Laidlaw."

"Well," she lowered her voice dramatically, "when he drove past me, he was *smiling*." Mrs. Martha D. sat back and shook her head. "No good will come of this."

Shirl caught my eye in the mirror, tilting her head and raising an eyebrow. I knew what she meant. Like it or not, Mrs. Martha D.'s pronouncements often proved true. I hoped in this case she'd be wrong. I knew all too well that ten years ago, it wasn't always a good thing to see Mac Laidlaw smiling.

The roar of the blow dryer put an end to further conversation, and when Shirl finished up, I paid her and left. I stood outside and glanced up and down the quietly prosperous main street, concern squirming unpleasantly in my gut. We had a good thing going in the town, and we didn't need anyone—CFA or otherwise—coming in and stirring things up.

Which Mac Laidlaw proceeded to do as early as the next afternoon. I was in my tiny town hall office, reviewing the minutes of the last council meeting, when Will knocked once and stuck his head in. Some of the older folk in town still shake their heads at a lady mayor with a male secretary, but times change, even here. Funny how that's harder to swallow than...other things.

"A Mr. Laidlaw here to see you," Will advised. "No appointment." Will was too young to have been very aware of Mac before he'd left town ten years ago, but his tone was disapproving.

I stifled a sigh. "Give me five minutes, then show him in." I tidied my desk, composed myself, and tried to feel pleasant when Mac walked in. The feeling didn't last long. He strode in smiling—no, *smirking*—and looked around the office as if he expected to get dirt on his shoes from the carpet.

"I had to come and see it for myself," he said, pulling one of the blue upholstered chairs closer to my desk and plunking himself down in it. "Lulu Coldbrook, Mayor?"

I returned a thin smile. "It's Louise, *J'nallan*," I said. Two could play the name game. "What brings you back to these parts? I'm sure your mother's happy to see you. Finally."

He'd narrowed his eyes when I called him by his given first name, but he let it pass. "Very happy," he said briefly. "But let's not waste time. I'm here with a business proposition."

"For me, or for the town?"

He grinned, a toothy, wolfish grin, and leaned forward, elbows on knees. "For the town. Louise. What if I told you I had a sure-fire plan to put this place on the map? Make it one of the biggest tourist attractions in Canada?"

My pulse pounded in my ears. *It's worse than I thought.* I pasted on a smile. "What do you mean?"

His smile was predatory, as if he had me on the hook, and now wanted me to dangle for a bit.

"What do you say we go out to dinner, and I'll tell you all about it? I saw a decent-looking restaurant on the way over here—Carmel's? Any good?"

I nodded. "That's Carmel MacIntyre—well, she's Donovan now—we went to school with her, remember? It's an excellent restaurant. But can't you just explain what you mean?"

Mac Laidlaw leaned back in the chair and

shook his head with a self-satisfied air. "The least you owe me is dinner out," he said pointedly.

I could have argued the implication that our breakup had been *my* fault, but I didn't have the energy. "All right, dinner at Carmel's it is. But not on the town's tab."

He stood and stuck his hands in his pockets. "Absolutely not. This is my show all the way. I'll meet you there at—6?"

"See you then."

He swaggered out and I frowned at his back as it disappeared. *My show all the way.* I didn't like the sound of that.

Mac was nursing a whiskey when I arrived at six o'clock on the dot. I'd timed my arrival very carefully, to avoid waiting for him (looking anxious) or making him wait for me (causing annoyance). I had promised myself I would play nice with Mac Laidlaw, at least until I knew exactly what he had planned for my peaceful, prosperous, and necessarily secretive little town.

He smiled and stood up to pull out my chair. He'd changed out of the suit he'd worn earlier and into a soft brown tweed sport jacket, crisp white shirt, and khakis. I was glad I'd dressed up in the blue dress I'd worn to Millie O'Handley's wedding last summer.

"You look great, Louise," Mac said. "Thanks for coming."

Okay, we were doing polite names.

"Thanks for the invitation, Mac," I said. "Let's order, and then you can fill me in on these big plans of yours."

The waiter offered us wine, which we both accepted, and I ordered the roast chicken dinner. Mac chose a steak with baked potato.

He looked around the crowded, well-appointed restaurant. "Town seems like it's doing pretty well," he observed. "I've been investigating since I left your office. Most of Cape Breton isn't in half the shape this place is." He didn't make it a question, but I knew it was.

I sipped wine and smiled. "We've got a good town council and quite a few folks commuting to decent jobs elsewhere," I said, "and of course, an excellent mayor." *And a secret industry you wouldn't believe.*

Mac grinned. "Of course. You're obviously doing a fine job. But wouldn't you love to see the place *really* take off? Look at the tourism industry in PEI. Cape Breton could have that, you know, if we had something central, something really big, to draw more people here in the first place."

"Don't tell me you've written the next *Anne of Green Gables*?"

"Ha!" Mac guffawed and swigged wine. "Nope, writing was never my strong suit. But I've just signed a deal that might be almost as big. You ever heard of The Bama Llama Club?"

"Kids' show on tv?" I asked, the name ringing a slightly familiar bell. Anthropomorphic alpacas? They sang, danced, and had adventures in exotic places.

Mac triggered a finger at me. "Only the third biggest kids' show in Canada and growing. This fall they're launching a line of books, a ton of merchandise, and there's talk of a movie." He leaned across the table and lowered his voice. "*Pixar*" he whispered significantly.

"So you're part of this? Sounds like a great investment." I couldn't see where this was going, or what it had to do with us.

"Honey, I can spot the winners. That's how I got where I am," he said, sitting back again. Smugness practically seeped out of his pores. "But look, I want to give back to my roots. When this opportunity came up, I latched right on to it."

I was going to scream pretty soon, if he didn't get to the point. "And that opportunity is—?"

Mac Laidlaw grinned like he was giving me the best news I'd ever heard. "A Bama Llama Club theme park. Right here on Cape Breton Island. Right *here* in this town. It's going to be bigger than Canada's Wonderland, and the whole town—this whole island—hell, this whole *province*—is going to reap the benefits." He leaned back to let the waitress set our dinner plates down. "And you'll have Mac Laidlaw to thank."

Somehow, I got through that dinner. The chicken tasted like sawdust, the potatoes like

168

glue. I couldn't even touch the cherry cobbler. There was nothing wrong with the cooking—it was all me, and the overwhelming panic that had blossomed in my chest at Mac's words.

My mind raced as I pushed food around on my plate. If he tried to build a theme park here, everything would be ruined. *Ruined.* And the repercussions would go far beyond the damage to the town. If the secret we guarded so closely and faithfully got out...

I pretended interest but cautioned Mac that I couldn't make a decision this big on my own. There'd be issues of land availability, zoning, permits...his disappointment and puzzlement at my lack of enthusiasm were evident, but surprisingly, he didn't press me too hard. He picked up the bill, we shook hands, and I thanked him for the dinner and his interest.

Then I raced home, changed my clothes, and high-tailed it to go see the real Mayor.

Yes, I am officially the Mayor of the town. Duly elected by the people and all that. But everyone who mattered knew there were two of us running things, and since we couldn't pronounce his name, we called him the Mayor, too. It seemed to make him happy, so it stuck.

I drove my ancient Honda out the old highway until I reached the turnoff for the long-abandoned Harbourside Mine site. The road was gated, but I quickly punched the code into my special remote and the dilapidated gate swung aside on surprisingly smooth hinges. I drove through and the gate swung closed behind me. The road itself appeared to be cracked and pocked with potholes, but I knew that was all illusion and sped along it smoothly at normal speed.

I swung around the old mine office building and parked behind it. Not that I really thought anyone—particularly Mac Laidlaw—was going to follow me out here, but why take chances?

Like the gate, the door of the mine office building looked deceptively ramshackle, secured with a rusted padlock that apparently hadn't been opened in decades. The Mayor once told me that the best illusions build on the truth. So there was indeed a door, but it was masked with as much skill as the roadway. It opened easily when I keyed in the code. Since dusk had fallen, low guidelights glowed on the floor, although by now I probably could have walked the hallway to the elevator with my eyes closed. I hurried along, passed through an illusory wall, and took the cheerily-lit elevator into the bowels of the mine.

When the doors opened, I smiled at the short, grinning person who waited to greet me. Her flawless skin was a pale lilac colour, and larger-than-human violet eyes regarded me with affection. Although she usually stood only a little over four feet tall, she seemed taller tonight, which was confirmed when she leaned in to hug me and came almost to my chin. I returned the hug and then held her at arm's length.

"Eske, did you grow?"

The petite alien grinned and extended a foot for my examination. She wore a pair of stiletto heels in what must have been at least a size ten to accommodate her sizable feet.

"Conrad found zem for me," she said in that weird accent that always sounded sort of Baltic to me. "Are zey not wonderful?"

I raised an eyebrow. "High heels might not be the best human fashion statement for you to adopt," I said. "Women around the world have been wrecking their legs and backs wearing them for decades."

She laughed, a high, glittery sound. "I must take my fun where I can find it, yes? And I promise not to wear zem more than I should. Now, what brings you?"

I remembered the seriousness of my errand with a pang. "I have to see the Mayor. We have a problem."

Eske became all business. She raised a spindly arm and spoke into a small device embedded in the back of her hand. I couldn't follow the rapid-fire alien language, although over the years I'd learned to speak it—a little, and badly. A reply must have emerged in her earpiece because she took my arm. "Let's go," she said. "He's in his office."

We hurried down a short hallway, so technologically advanced from the old mine tunnel it had once been that it was difficult to believe we were underground. Gleaming silver walls arched gracefully overhead, and the floor seemed to be the same material, just a few shades darker in colour. Guidelights ran along the seam between floor and walls, and a glowing strip followed the peak of the arch above our heads.

The corridor opened out into a large room with a low ceiling. Two aliens tapped and clicked at computer terminals. One looked up and raised a hand in greeting, and I smiled and nodded back. The room resembled the bridge of a starship, from television or movies. Unsurprising, since that's exactly what it was. The surprising part was how close human imagination had come. This was the ship that had crashed here eight years ago, throwing the town into upheaval, fear, and ultimately, prosperity.

The door to the Mayor's office opened as we approached, and he stepped out to greet us. Taller than all the other aliens by almost a foot, he was still slightly shorter than I am. His colouring was violet to Eske's lilac, his eyes a pale green. He extended a hand for me to shake, which I did, and then I clapped my hands to my shoulders and he did the same to his own, which was their own form of greeting.

"Mayor Loueezze," he said warmly, his accent thicker than Eske's. "What brings you out at zis time of night?"

"Trouble, I'm afraid," I said. "We need to talk."

He stood back from the door and motioned me inside. Eske said, "Call if you need me," and crossed to her own computer terminal on the ship's bridge.

Inside the Mayor's office, he sat behind his desk and I took one of the two seats facing it. I sighed involuntarily as the chair automatically adjusted to fit my height and body, making it the most comfortable seat I'd ever experienced. Sensors noted the tension that had settled between my shoulder blades and automatically began a light massage.

As succinctly as possible, I brought the Mayor up to speed on Mac Laidlaw's plans to put our little Cape Breton town on the map. As he listened attentively, his wide, high brow creased with worry lines just as a human's might have. If he'd had eyebrows, they would have been pulled down and together by the time I finished my tale.

"Zis is indeed unfortunate," he said, tapping the tips of his long, slender fingers together. "We are still at least five years away from completing repairs. To risk discovery now..." He let the words trail off and I nodded. Although there were times I wished the aliens would never fix their ship and leave us, I knew that practicality demanded it. And, we could keep the town prosperous and healthy for decades on the technology they'd already shared. We carefully administered it all through a blind trust and several dummy corporations, filing patents cautiously and occasionally to avoid setting any alarm bells ringing. Our economic good fortune was already spreading slowly to the rest of the island. Eventually we would enter a new boom era.

But not with Mac Laidlaw's theme park bumbling in and causing havoc.

"How am I going to dissuade him?" I asked. "I don't suppose you have any technology that would affect his memory, make him forget this whole plan?"

The Mayor sighed. "Unfortunately, no. We are very good at projecting ze illusions, but not directly affecting ze brain. And zat is probably a good zing. We might have been tempted to use it when we crashed, and our mutually beneficial partnership might never have come to pass."

"True enough." Even the chair's massage couldn't entirely alleviate the tension in my back. I stood. "Well, think on it, will you? And I'll do the same. Surely one of us will come up with a way to stop this."

He nodded and stood, too. "I will put our best minds on it," he promised, coming around the desk to open the door for me. "And zank you very much for letting me know what is afoot."

"Maybe you could speed up your repairs?" I said, although I hated to suggest it. "A theme park will take a while to build; it's not going to happen overnight. You might be out of here before the risk of detection becomes too great."

"Zat is most zoughtful of you, but what if your Mac Laidlaw decides zat zis site would be ze best place to build ze park? No," he shook his head, "even if we could proceed faster, it might not be fast enough. We need anozzer solution."

I nodded. "Then we'll have to find one."

I just had no idea how.

I called an emergency meeting of the town council the next morning. Only Evie MacMullin couldn't make it, because she was out of town, but everyone else showed up within an hour of getting the phone call. Even Shirl cancelled an appointment to come in. We gathered in the board room, six of us around the big mahogany table.

As soon as I mentioned Mac Laidlaw's name, Charlie McKee rolled his eyes. "I heard he was back, shooting the drag in his big car just the same as when he was a teenager," he said. "Only difference is, then it was a ten-year-old Caddy, now it's an extended wheelbase Audi A8." Not hard to tell Charlie ran the biggest garage in town.

"He thinks he has the world by the tail," I said, "but here's the problem. He wants to bring a big development here, and he won't be easily dissuaded. He sees himself as the town saviour—maybe even for the whole island."

Harold Christmas, the high school chemistry teacher, crossed his arms. "And if we tell him we don't need saving?"

I shook my head. "He won't care. We'll need something pretty persuasive to make him back away from this."

Sally Donovan leaned forward, tapping long, finely manicured nails on the polished wood of the table. "We might have to take it to The Mayor." She smiled at me. "I mean, the other mayor."

"I already did. Went out to see him last night. He didn't have any suggestions, but he said he'd think on it."

"Well, we can't let Mac Laidlaw have his way," Shirl protested. "It's our town, after all, not his. He went his own way years ago. The nerve, thinking he can come back and just take over."

"Maybe his mother can stop him," Sally said, but I think we all knew as soon as the words were out that it was a hopeless suggestion. Mild Mrs. Laidlaw hadn't managed to exert much influence over her son when he was a boy, so it was unlikely she'd do any better now.

"We'll start by refusing to grant the permits," Harold said. "Where does he want to put the thing?"

"He hasn't said yet, but I can think of two big, flat, suitable possibilities," I said glumly.

Charlie's eyes went wide. "The old quarry, or the old mine site."

I shrugged as a ripple of apprehension circled the room. "That'd be my guess."

Sally turned to me. "Can't you talk to him? You knew Mac Laidlaw better than anyone else in town." Then she blushed to the roots of her hair. "Sorry, dear," she added, reaching across

176

the table to pat my hand.

I shook my head. "It's all right. It's true, although I hope I have more sense now."

"You had sense, it just took you some time to act on it," Sally said staunchly. "After all, you *didn't* marry him."

No, I hadn't married Mac Laidlaw, but it had been a close thing. And somehow, after all these years, I still felt responsible for him.

"We'll try the permits thing," I told them, "and if that doesn't work, well, we'll think of something. See what you can come up with. We'll meet again after I've talked to Mac, and I'll let you know how it goes."

"What the hell is wrong with you people?"

Mac Laidlaw glanced around the coffee shop, apparently realizing how loudly he'd spoken. He caught a few curious glances and met them with an affable grin, running a hand over his hair and calming himself with a visible effort.

I took a sip of coffee and a breath. "Look, Mac, we appreciate your wanting to help out. It's just that what you're proposing is going to change things too much. We're quiet, we're doing fine, and we like it this way. We don't want to turn into a tourist trap. That's why the council won't grant the permits. It's that simple."

Mac glared at me, lips pressed together in a thin white line. When he spoke, his voice was low again. "You're behind this, aren't you?

177

You've got them all turned against me—"

I held up a hand. "This isn't personal. No grudges here."

"Hah." He sat back in his chair, eyeing me with disbelief. Then he shrugged. "I guess we'll do this the hard way, then. I'll go to the province. I've got friends in high places. I'll get those permits one way or the other."

"Even if the town doesn't want this? Even if the people say no?"

He smiled, but it was the kind of smile that would have made Mrs. Martha D. even more worried. "You just don't know what's good for you," he said. "You'll come around to my way of thinking in the end."

Then he stood, tossing a twenty-dollar bill on the table to pay for the coffee and raisin biscuits we'd had. "This is going to happen, Louise. You made a fool of me once. It's not going to happen again."

He stormed out, and I sat sipping my coffee, waiting for the pounding in my head to subside. I'd been wrong about one thing, anyway. This was definitely personal.

Shirl from The Hair Net slid into the chair Mac Laidlaw had vacated. "Seemed like that went well."

I blew out a sigh. "If I needed any reminding about why I broke it off with that man—"

She reached over and patted my hand. "Always was stubborn as a pit mule, that one," she said. "And he cares too much about appearances. Can't lose face."

"That's for—" I broke off as an idea hit me.

The best illusions build on the truth.

Shirl stared at me quizzically. Then a slow smile spread across her face. "You've got an idea."

I put my coffee cup down carefully, still thinking. "I just might," I said, "but I'm going to need some help." Time to go see the Mayor again, to find out if what I had in mind was even possible.

Two days later, just after dusk, I stood by the gate to the old quarry, waiting for Mac Laidlaw. I'd caught the undertone of malicious satisfaction in his voice when I'd called and asked him to meet me here, to discuss his theme park idea further. I knew he'd been calling in favours from around the province since our meeting at the coffee shop. Now he thought we were going to cave to his demands.

I sent a quick text to Eske. The aliens had easily adopted some of our technology—like cell phones—and we'd spent the last day hauling some of their technology over here from the old mine and caching it behind quarry debris. *All set?*

Ready on this end, came the quick reply. *We're monitoring.*

We were not planning to cave.

Headlights pricked around the corner and I dropped my cell phone into my pocket. The Mayor had assured me their tech was equal to the task, and I trusted him, but my heart beat a nervous tattoo in my chest. This would only work if Mac Laidlaw was still the man I thought he was.

His big car pulled up next to my little hybrid and he rolled down the window. "Strange place for a meeting, Mayor."

I shrugged. "Am I wrong in assuming you'd consider this a possible site for the theme park?"

"You've changed your mind, then?"

"Let's take a stroll," I said. I already had the gate open and Mac left his car to join me. We started into the shadowy, three-sided cavern of the abandoned quarry, my flashlight picking out a path ahead of us.

Mac peered into the half-dark, presumably imagining Bama Llama rides and Bama Llama snacks and Bama Llama merchandise everywhere.

I felt a little sorry for the guy. But as I saw the swagger in his step growing more pronounced the farther we went, I got over it.

"Look, Mac, we can't let you build a theme park in this town," I said, stopping as we neared the rusted trailer that had once served as quarry office.

He turned to me with a frown. "What? I thought things had changed."

"They have not."

He laughed bemusedly, looking around. "Then why are we here?"

"Because I have to show you something," I said. "The reason you can't build a Bama

Llama park here."

That was the cue, and I hoped Eske had heard it or I was about to look like an idiot. Then the air in front of me took on a sort of shimmery overlay and Mac Laidlaw's eyes grew really, really wide. He stumbled back a couple of steps, and his mouth worked silently.

"Wha—" he squeaked.

If things were working correctly—and I assumed from his reaction they were—Mac Laidlaw was now seeing me as an alien. Not an alien like Eske and the Mayor, of course—we were protecting secrets, not giving them away. We'd devised an illusion that made me look something like an eight-foot-tall crayfish in a toga-like robe. Kind of pulp sci-fi, but impressive.

"This...is my true form, Mac," I said, trying not to sound too dramatic.

"Wha—" he choked.

"I know this is hard to swallow, but about half of the people in town actually look like this. We're aliens who crash-landed here a long time ago, and we've just—well, camouflaged ourselves to fit in. But we can't risk being discovered. You used to watch *The X-Files*, Mac. You know what the government would do to us."

"Bu—bu—"

"There's our ship," I said, gesturing to the back of the quarry. On cue, a partially-destroyed spaceship shimmered into view. "We keep it cloaked, but it's there."

181

We'd based the shape off an old sci-fi movie, but I doubted Mac would recognize it from this angle.

Mac's throat worked as he swallowed a few times, looking between the spaceship and me. He seemed to get hold of himself, staring at me intently.

"Louise? Is that really you?"

I sighed theatrically. "You can see why I couldn't go through with marrying you. It was a nice dream, for a while. But—it would never have worked. Sooner or later, you would have figured it out."

Mac put a hand to his forehead as if taking his own temperature. His face was pale in the emerging moonlight, his eyes wild. "But...but...half the town? Who?"

I shook my head. "That's a take-it-to-the-grave secret, Mac. You know the old saying. If I told you, I'd have to—"

He staggered a couple of steps back. "Wait. I'll—I'll tell. You can't do this. You're—you're not even human!"

I laughed. The spaceship winked out and the shimmer around me disappeared. I did a slow turn. "Tell? Tell what? Tell who? You think anyone will believe I'm not exactly what I say I am? You of all people *know* the illusion is so real that you could kiss me and—" I leaned toward him, puckering up, and he shied away like a frightened horse.

"But the ship—" He turned to where the wrecked spaceship had apparently been. "It's there. I—I could bring someone and they'd find it. I'd have proof."

I stepped closer to Mac and laid a hand on his cold, clammy cheek. "Trust me, Mac. You could bring someone. But they won't find a ship. They won't see any aliens. And you will look like an idiot."

He cringed back from my touch. He seemed to rally, crossing his arms and raising his chin.

"All right, I won't tell anyone. I'll just come here and build the park anyway. How are you going to stop me?"

I'd thought it might go this way. I closed my eyes and shook my head slowly, allowing myself a theatrical little laugh. "Mac. Didn't you hear me? We're *aliens*. We can do things with our minds—well, watch."

I turned to look back at our cars.

Bright light erupted near the gate, a white-hot luminescence I had to squint against. Mac threw an arm up to shield his eyes and yelped.

"What the—"

As the light dimmed, he ran toward his car, half-stumbling. I followed at a slower pace, knowing what he'd find. Four flat tires and an engine that wouldn't start...at least until he'd had the alternator replaced. Harold and Charlie would be back in hiding behind a couple of leftover stone slabs near the gate, probably giggling childishly over the fun of disabling the car and burning some magnesium from Harold's classroom.

When I reached the car, Mac was struggling

to get the engine to turn over. I opened the passenger door and leaned in. "I can drive you back into town," I offered. "But this is just a taste of how we'll stop the park. A *small* taste," I emphasized. "Like, appetizer-sized. I'm sorry, Mac, but it will never be built. Permits, investigations, the ruin of your reputation...it doesn't matter. No park is going here."

Mac stopped turning the key and slowly let his head sink forward until it rested on the steering wheel.

"Go to hell, Louise," he said finally, "or whoever you really are. I'll walk back."

I let him.

To give him his due, Mac Laidlaw stayed in town for Mother's Day, and I heard he took his mother out to brunch at Carmel's. I didn't see him again after our night at the quarry. I held my breath for a few days after he'd left in his big Audi, wondering if our little piece of theatre had worked, but apparently it did. Last I heard, he was starting up a Bama Llama theme park out in Alberta somewhere. I still wonder if someone will eventually show up at the old quarry, poking around for a spaceship that isn't there, but I don't lose too much sleep over it.

You should see the latest piece of tech the Mayor gave me last week. Well, you will see it, when it hits the marketplace. You just won't know where it came from.

Come-from-aways—they're not so bad, once

you get to know them. Sometimes it's the home-grown ones you have to watch.

*****

Sherry D. Ramsey is a Canadian science fiction and fantasy writer, editor, publisher, creativity addict and self-confessed Internet geek. When she's not writing, she reads, gardens, procrastinates on social media, and consumes more chocolate and coffee than is likely good for her. Her books and stories range across fantasy, urban fantasy, mystery, and science fiction. She's been Chief Moderator and Writer Wrangler at the Story Forge Writers Group for (gulp) twenty years.

Sherry started this story a long time ago and was re-inspired to finish it for inclusion in this anthology. This is precisely why Sherry never deletes unfinished stories from her hard drive, no matter how ancient their electrons become.

Visit Sherry online at her website, www.sherrydramsey.com, and keep up with her much more pithy musings on Twitter @sdramsey.